"Kathi Macias has written a warm, tender story about a widow with two young children struggling to survive a homeless winter. Your heart will ache for this little family as they shuffle back and forth between street and shelter. This touching tale of enduring faith and eternal love will not only bring you to tears but leave you smiling at the end."

—MARGARET BROWNLEY, *New York Times* best-selling author
of "The Brides of Last Chance Ranch" series

"Kathi Macias does it again! In *Unexpected Christmas Hero*, she tugs at the heart . . . and then pulls some more for a heart-wrenching story about all aspects of humanity. This story shows how acts of faith from the most unexpected person can make a monumental difference in the lives of those who have been in the deepest, darkest trenches of life."

—DEBBY MAYNE, author of *Sweet Baklava*
and the upcoming "Class Reunion" series

KATHI MACIAS

NEW HOPE
PUBLISHERS
Gospel-Centered. Missions-Driven.

New Hope® Publishers
P. O. Box 12065
Birmingham, AL 35202-2065
NewHopeDigital.com
New Hope Publishers is a division of WMU®.

Library of Congress Cataloging-in-Publication Data

Macias, Kathi, 1948-
  Unexpected Christmas hero / Kathi Macias.
    p. cm.
  ISBN 978-1-59669-354-8 (sc)
  1. Christmas stories. I. Title.
  PS3563.I42319U54 2012
  813'.54--dc23

                              2012026202

Cover Designer: Michel Le
Photo: Used by Permission.
Interior designer: Glynese Northam

ISBN-10: 1-59669-354-1
ISBN-13: 978-1-59669-354-8

N124107 • 1012 • 3M1

OTHER TITLES BY
Kathi Macias

⊰≈⊱

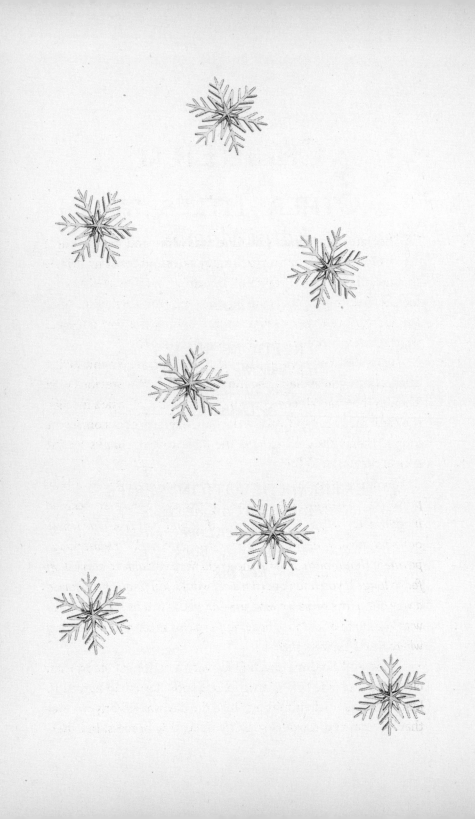

CHAPTER 1

The late November sunshine was thin and tepid, but a welcome interruption to the gray skies and constant drizzle that usually hung over the small Washington town of Riverview for the better part of eight or nine months each year. Josie Meyers shivered as she stood in line behind her two children, waiting their turn for a free Thanksgiving meal.

Tears bit her eyes at the memory of past Thanksgiving celebrations, particularly the most recent one the previous year. Though they had all been grieving the passing of Josie's mother, they still managed to turn the day into a festive occasion, as the four of them gathered around the table to give thanks for the spread that awaited them.

Sam, she thought. *You stood there that day, offering a brief prayer of thanksgiving to a God I'm not sure you even believed in, and never let on for a moment that you hadn't a clue where our next meal would come from or how we'd make the mortgage payment that month. How in the world were you able to carry it off for so long? If you hadn't gotten sick, would you finally have found a way out of the mess we were in — or would you be standing here with the three of us now, begging for a hot meal and wondering where we'd sleep tonight?*

Jacob and Susanna shuffled forward a couple of steps, each clutching a plastic tray in their bare hands. Josie had agreed to let them remove their mittens since the day was slightly warmer than normal and it would simplify the eating process, but she'd cautioned them to tuck the hand coverings securely in their jacket pockets as they would need them again by evening.

Josie could smell the food now, and her mouth watered despite the sadness that clutched her insides and regularly threatened to emotionally disembowel her. They'd lost it all. Everything! First her mother, then her husband . . . and finally their home. *Not to mention our dignity*, she thought, refusing to let the tears flow from her eyes onto her cheeks. *Will there ever be an end to this?*

She watched as plates of turkey and potatoes, dressing and cranberry sauce, plus slices of pumpkin pie and cups of cold drinks, were placed on her children's trays. Should she offer to help Susanna carry hers? After all, she was only five. And yet she was an independent five and did not appreciate what she called "being treated like a baby." Restraining herself from her usual hovering, Josie allowed her children to maneuver themselves to a nearby table. Though Susanna's tray wobbled a bit, she managed just fine. Josie sighed with relief and placed her own tray on the long white table before seating herself on a rickety plastic chair between her offspring.

"Do we need to pray again?" Susanna asked, her wide blue eyes peering upward at her mother. "The lady said they already prayed and blessed the food before we came in."

Josie knew she should set a good example and offer a prayer herself, but her heart wasn't in it. Though she appreciated the food, it was hard to feel grateful these days.

Before she could say anything, seven-year-old Jacob, who had taken quite naturally to his new role as man of the house — *even though we don't have a house*, Josie groused silently — closed his eyes and folded his hands. "Thank You for the food, God," he prayed. "And thanks for everyone who came and fixed it for us. And . . ." He paused before adding, " . . . and please give us and everybody here somewhere warm to sleep tonight. Amen."

The tears Josie had been holding back slipped out onto her cheeks, and she kept her head bowed in an effort to hide them. How had she ended up with children who trusted God and prayed when she'd been so uncommitted and casual about taking them to church regularly? Then again, her own mother had taken her to church faithfully, and look how Josie's faith had deteriorated. Her mother had cautioned her against marrying an unbeliever, but she hadn't listened. They'd been in love, after all, and he'd been such a loving husband and father, a wonderful provider . . . until the economy collapsed and his job along with it.

How did everything get so bad . . . so fast? How is it possible that our happy, comfortable suburban life disintegrated and left us with nothing more than heartbreaking memories and a daily struggle just to survive?

"It's OK, Mom," Jacob said, patting Josie's hand. "We have a great dinner today."

Josie swiped at the remaining tears on her face and nodded at her son, forcing a smile. "We do, don't we?" she said, determined to encourage the two people she loved most in all the world. "And it looks delicious, doesn't it?"

"It sure looks good, Mommy," Susanna chirped, picking up her fork and plunging it into her mashed potatoes. "I just love potatoes and gravy."

Josie nodded again. "I know you do," she said, a bittersweet joy flooding her heart as she watched her children eat one of the few balanced meals they'd had in many weeks.

As she took a first bite from her own plate, she noticed an older man in a tattered green jacket lower himself into a seat directly across from her. Without being obvious, she studied the wrinkles that lined his face and the gray hair and beard that framed it. She imagined he was about the age her father would have been if he were still alive.

"Happy Thanksgiving," the man said, a smile spreading across his countenance that seemed to erase many of his wrinkles and set his brown eyes to sparkling. "This is quite a meal they've cooked up here, isn't it?"

From the corner of her eye, Josie saw her protective son sizing up the stranger who had just invaded their space. Apparently the man passed inspection because Jacob returned his smile and said, "Yep. It's great!"

Susanna stuffed another forkful of potatoes in her mouth as she silently eyed their new tablemate.

"I'm Rick," he said, extending his hand across the table toward Jacob.

"Do you have a last name?" Jacob said, accepting the handshake.

The man smiled. "I do, but I prefer to be called Rick."

Jacob smiled. "OK . . . Rick. I'm Jacob, and this is my mom, Josie Meyers, and my sister, Susanna."

Rick turned his attention toward Josie. "Hello, Josie Meyers," he said before sliding his eyes toward the little girl who stared at him intently. "And hello, Susanna. Nice to meet you both."

Susanna's eyes widened and she nodded. Josie knew she should offer her hand but just couldn't bring herself to do it. "Nice to meet you too," she mumbled, hoping the man didn't intend to carry on a conversation throughout the entire meal. If there was one thing Josie clung to at homeless shelters or soup kitchens it was anonymity. She had to divulge enough personal and family information each time she filled out a stack of paperwork at yet another social services agency. But it was all necessary if she was to continue receiving even a miniscule amount of support each month and, eventually, some sort of regular housing. Meanwhile, they supplemented their tiny income by eating free meals anywhere they could and sleeping in shelters whenever there were beds available. But Josie kept to herself and tried to teach her children to do the same. It wasn't easy, though, especially with friendly, outgoing Jacob.

So much like Sam . . .

She shook off the thought and returned to her meal, hoping the man would take the hint and allow them to eat in silence.

"Were you in the war?" Jacob asked.

Josie's head jerked up, and she glanced from her son to the man named Rick, who was smiling once again. She hadn't noticed until this moment that the tattered green jacket he wore was most likely some sort of military issue, though it looked like it had survived one too many battles.

"I sure was," Rick said. "Vietnam. Ever hear of it?"

Jacob nodded. "My dad told me about it. That was a long time ago. Were you a hero?"

Rick laughed, which quickly morphed into a cough. It was obvious he struggled to get it under control. At last he said, "You're right, Jacob. It was a very long time ago. I was a young man then, in my early twenties. And no, I wasn't a hero."

Jacob's eyes widened as he no doubt calculated how old Rick must be by now. The numbers rolled in Josie's mind, too, as she realized how difficult it would be for a man of his age to be living on the streets. *And how sad,* she thought. *To have served his country and end up homeless . . .*

Once again she forced herself away from her thoughts. This was no time to go sentimental on everyone. She had to stay strong for her children, even though she questioned what that meant and how to do it.

"Well," said Rick, shoving his chair back and standing to his feet, "I think I've eaten about all I can." He shrugged. "Just not too hungry today, I guess." He glanced at Jacob. "Think you could help me out and eat this here piece of pumpkin pie for me? I'd sure hate to see it go to waste."

Doubt crisscrossed the boy's features, but at last he nodded. "Sure. I'd be glad to help you out."

Rick set the small white paper plate with the pie and whipped cream on Jacob's tray, nodded a quick farewell to the three of them, and then picked up his own tray. "Enjoy the rest of your day," he said before turning and walking away.

"That was nice of him," Jacob said, his eyes fixed on Rick's departing form.

Josie nodded. It was obvious that even Jacob seemed to understand that Rick wasn't really full and could easily have eaten the pie.

"Did the nice man give us a present, Mommy?" Susanna asked.

Josie looked down at her daughter and offered her a wobbly smile. "He sure did, sweetheart," she said. "A Thanksgiving present."

Susanna smiled and nodded, her dangling legs swinging beneath her chair. "I like that," she said, and went back to her meal.

* * *

"I'm sleepy, Mommy."

Josie's heart constricted at her daughter's statement. Though grateful for the filling meal they'd had a few hours earlier, the afternoon had worn on with little hope of a warm place to spend the night. It was Thanksgiving Day, and the end of the month was near. For a homeless family, that translated into not enough money left from their welfare check to rent a room.

Six more days, Josie calculated. *Six more days until we get another check and I can be assured of getting my kids off the street, at least during the coldest nights.*

She shivered. Temperatures dropped considerably after dark, but she knew it wasn't nearly as cold yet as it would be in the next month or two. She prayed this particular winter wasn't an exceptionally cold one, with rare periods of ice and snow. Rain was bad enough.

At least we don't have that tonight, she thought, peering up at the faint stars twinkling overhead. Memories of growing up on the family farm in the eastern part of the state, where stars blazed like beacons, tugged at her heart. Here in town those same stars shone dimly at best.

She sighed. They'd waited around at the soup kitchen as long as they could after they'd finished their meal, hoping to hear of a nearby shelter for the night. But as evening shadows grew longer, her hopes dimmed. How she had prayed for a miracle, that somehow God would provide a safe spot for them, even at the last moment, but it hadn't happened. And why should she be surprised? It wasn't as if God had been in the business of listening to or answering her prayers lately.

Standing at the street corner with a child on each side, waiting for the light to change, she closed her eyes, remembering how desperately she and so many others had prayed for God to spare her mother when her heart rebelled and seemed determined to stop pumping. But to no avail. Within weeks she was gone, and Josie struggled to accept the commonly repeated statement that "at least her suffering is over and she's happy now."

Really? Did that mean she wasn't happy when she was here with her family? Josie had wanted to ask that question but never did. And while she was still reeling from that loss, a routine doctor's visit revealed the cancer that was ravaging Sam's body.

"There's little we can do," the doctor announced. "It's very aggressive, and it's already invaded nearly every part of his body, including his bones and organs. I wish I had better news."

So do I, she remembered thinking. But he hadn't. No one had. And so she had watched her beloved partner melt away before her eyes, as she agonized over how she would get her children through it all.

The very thought of being a single parent had terrified her, particularly since she'd never worked or taken care of the bills. She'd left all that to Sam . . . and she'd trusted him to take care of it. How foolish she had been!

"Mommy, the light changed."

The familiar voice reached her at the same time she felt the tug on her right hand. Opening her eyes, she glanced down at her daughter, whose upturned face was already flushed from the cold night air. She had to get them to safety and warmth, quickly. The only place she knew that was nearby and even remotely fit that description was the spot behind the cleaners across the street. Hopefully no one else had already beaten them to it.

Smiling reassuringly, she turned her face forward and stepped into the street, gently tugging her children along with her. At least they had warm jackets and blankets, and it wasn't raining. If they huddled together, they'd make it until morning.

❄ ❄ ❄

"Ma'am?"

Josie started at the unexpected male voice. She had been so relieved to find the little corner behind the cleaners vacant and was busily spreading blankets and fixing a makeshift bed for herself and the children when she realized they weren't alone after all.

Her heart raced as she turned toward the voice, straining in the darkness to identify the tall figure that stood just a few feet away. *Oh God, please,* she prayed silently, too frightened to remember that she was angry with the Almighty, *protect us!*

The man took a step closer, and instinctively she grabbed her children and pulled them close. "What do you want?" she asked, her fear obvious in her shaky voice.

A cough preceded his answer. "It's me, Rick," he said at last, taking another step, close enough now that his features were almost recognizable. "From Thanksgiving dinner, remember?"

She could nearly make out the ratty green jacket then, as Jacob exclaimed, "Rick! You're the one who gave me your pie."

Rick chuckled. "Yes, I am. And I sure do thank you for helping me out and eating it for me. Like I said, I can't abide wasting food."

Josie's heart thrummed against her rib cage. Did she dare trust this man? Was he truly a friend, or had he followed them here to harm them? The last few months on the streets had made her skittish of everyone.

"Look, Mom," Jacob said, pulling loose from Josie's grasp and looking up at her. "It's the man who gave me his pie."

Josie forced a smile but pulled Jacob back into her embrace. "Yes, I see that," she said, trying to calm her voice as she shifted her gaze to the man who claimed to be named Rick. "Thank you very much for that. I appreciate your kindness."

"Mom said you gave us a Thanksgiving present," Susanna said.

Rick chuckled again. "Well, I suppose I did."

"Why?" Susanna asked.

The man paused. "I guess because God has given me so much," he said, "and I just like to give back when I can."

He sounds like I used to . . . once, Josie thought. *Before the world caved in and taught me otherwise—and God abandoned us.*

"Well . . . thank you again," she forced herself to say. "But now my children and I need to get some sleep. Will you excuse us?"

17

"Actually, that's why I'm here," Rick said. "I spotted you crossing the street and realized you probably didn't know the soup kitchen opens their warehouse on Thanksgiving night so people can sleep there. They don't have a permit to do it except on special occasions, but tonight is one of them. If we hurry, we might still get in before it's full."

Josie's heart leapt. A warehouse? Somewhere to sleep inside, out of the elements and away from the dangers of the open street? Could it be possible?

"Mom," Jacob said, pulling away to look up at her once again, "I prayed that, remember? Before we had dinner, I asked God to give us all a place to sleep tonight. Not just us but the other people who were there too."

Even in the dim light Josie could tell her son's eyes were gleaming, and her own hope flickered a bit brighter too. Yes, he had prayed that, hadn't he? Was it just a coincidence? Did it even matter? There was a chance for a warm, safe place to sleep tonight! But they'd have to hurry.

Bending down to scoop up their belongings, she spoke as she worked. "Thank you again. It was kind of you to come and tell us."

"My pleasure," he said, leaning over to help Josie retrieve the blankets and sacks she had scattered on the ground just moments earlier. He coughed again and then said, "We'd better get going so we can be sure to get in before they close the doors for the night."

It wasn't until Josie found herself gripping Susanna's hand and hurrying to keep up with Rick and Jacob, who walked in front of her, that she realized she had taken a big chance by believing the word of a complete stranger and following after him. But he seemed harmless enough, and at least he was leading them in the direction of the soup kitchen where they'd met him earlier. Besides, at the moment it seemed the best option they had going for them.

CHAPTER 2

Josie nearly erupted into tears of relief when they arrived at the soup kitchen and were told they made it with a few minutes to spare.

"Head right in through that open door over there," said the smiling woman whose plump face made Josie think of her aunt Jeneen, who'd been gone for nearly ten years now. "We still have a half-dozen or so spaces left, and as soon as those are filled we'll lock up for the night." She glanced down at Jacob and Susanna, and her smile widened. "So glad you could join us. It's nice and warm in there, and we'll have donuts and apples for everybody in the morning."

"I love donuts," Susanna said, beaming up at the woman.

She leaned down and whispered, "So do I—more than I should, I'm afraid."

Susanna giggled, and the lady turned to greet two men who stood waiting to be admitted.

Rick led the way, the children happily following, as Josie took up the rear, mulling over how far they had fallen that she should be thrilled at the opportunity for her family to spend the night in a warehouse full of strangers. *Homeless people*, she reminded herself. *Like us.*

She pushed aside memories of stepping into each child's gaily decorated room to tuck them into bed before padding down the hall to join Sam in their own bedroom. On rare warm evenings they often sat outside on the adjoining terrace before retiring. Tonight she just wanted to get inside, out of the cold night air and away from the dangers of the streets.

Six more days, she reminded herself. *Only six more days and I'll have enough money to rent a room now and then — until the money runs out again.* She squeezed back tears and glanced around at their new surroundings.

"Mommy, look," Susanna cried, pulling on Josie's hand. "There's other kids here — like me. Can I play with them?"

Josie's heart squeezed at the sight of two little girls, seemingly younger than Susanna or possibly just smaller from having been on the streets longer. They sat on a spread-out blanket, one on each side of the woman who was no doubt their mother, and stared at Susanna, wide-eyed.

"Can I play with them, Mommy?" Susanna repeated.

Josie looked down at her. "Not now, sweetheart," she said. "It's late, and they'll be turning the lights down soon. We've been in shelters like this before, and you know what that means. We have to lie down and go to sleep."

Susanna's shoulders slumped, and the light in her blue eyes dimmed, but she nodded. "I know, Mommy." For just a moment Josie saw herself in her daughter — the soft blue eyes that could turn from sparkling to dim in an instant, the shoulder-length blonde hair that, though tangled and straggly, mirrored her own at that age. But it was the girl's defeated posture that most reminded Josie of herself at that instant.

"Here, Mom," Jacob offered, handing one end of their softest blanket to her. "I'll help you spread this out so we can get a spot while the lights are still on."

"Good plan," Rick said, ruffling Jacob's hair. "You all settle here. There's plenty of room, and it's near the heater."

Josie glanced at the space heaters set up around the room and realized how fortunate they were to find a place close by one of them. She quickly grabbed one end of the blanket that Jacob still held and helped him spread it out. When she looked up, Rick had wandered over to another corner of the room where it appeared the single men were gathered. As nice as he was, she was relieved he'd taken that initiative.

"Lights out in five minutes," a male voice called.

Josie and her little ones settled down on the blanket and took off their jackets to roll up as pillows. They had one more blanket to cover themselves with, and without words they snuggled close so it would spread across all three of them.

It didn't take long for all this to become a routine, Josie thought as she rested her head on her improvised pillow. *Just like heading for the spot behind the cleaners is our last resort when nothing better turns up. We're learning to survive, to live like street people . . . and I don't like it one bit.*

The lights went down then, and she clenched her teeth, shooting a silent prayer—more of a complaint, really—to the silent heavens above. *Did You hear that, God? I don't like any of this, not at all. Why did You let this happen to us?*

"Isn't this great, Mom?" Jacob whispered, his lips just inches from her ear. "I prayed for a place to sleep tonight   for everyone who was eating here today—and here we are."

Josie did her best to swallow the lump in her throat, even as Susanna laid her head on her mother's shoulder. "Yes," Josie said at last, "here we are. The three of us."

In moments her children's even breathing told her they had dropped off, while she lay on her back, staring up into the semidarkness and trying to ignore the hot tears that slid from her eyes, down her face, and into her ears and hair. What was to become of them? How long could they go on like this? Would they be able to survive until some sort of housing opened up for them? She'd visited every possible government agency and charitable organization, filled out more paperwork than she'd imagined existed in the entire world, and always the answer was the same: "We'll put you on the waiting list, Mrs. Meyers, but there are quite a few ahead of you."

And to think that just the year before she and Sam had fallen into bed at the end of Thanksgiving Day, moaning and groaning about having eaten far too much, knowing their children were already asleep in their rooms. Though Sam was aware they were in trouble, Josie had no idea. She had drifted off in her husband's arms, a false sense of security blanketing her from the reality that would explode into their lives in just a matter of months.

※ ※ ※

Karen had been involved in homeless-type ministries for nearly twenty years now, ever since her husband, John, died in a car accident, just months after they were married. So many had encouraged her to consider remarriage, as she was still young and had no children. But she felt as if that part of her life had ended with John. And because he'd wisely provided her with a sizeable life insurance policy as a wedding present, she was able to devote her life to serving God in whatever capacity He called her. Though even now, after almost two decades, she still had her moments when her heart ached for her beloved husband, she had found great joy and satisfaction in the life God had provided for her.

Serving Thanksgiving dinner at the soup kitchen was at the top of her favorites list. It had been a long day, beginning with cooking and preparing the food and then dishing it out to the long line of hungry recipients. After that there was the cleanup, and by the time that was finished she figured she might as well just stay and help welcome the stragglers who came looking for a warm night's sleep.

The little girl with the big blue eyes and a love for donuts had touched her heart in such a personal way. Even now, as she drove the few miles toward home, she smiled at the thought. If John had lived, would they have had a little girl like that? She sighed. As a teenager and then a college student in the years before she and John married, she always imagined herself with a little girl—or two or three. John had declared that he wanted a full house, "as many kids as possible." And he would have been a great father, she knew.

Just as I would have been a good mother, she assured herself. *But God had another plan—a better one, because He knows what's best for all of us.*

"She's a precious little girl, Lord," she whispered, her mind returning to the child who had caught her attention. "What could have happened to put that sweet family out on the street?" She sighed, as she pictured the three of them together. The boy appeared to be a couple of years older than his sister, and his hair and eyes were dark, rather than blond. It was apparent the girl had inherited her looks and coloring from her mother, and Karen couldn't help but think the boy must look like his father. But where was the man? Had he deserted them? Karen had heard nearly every heartbreaking story imaginable, so nothing surprised her. But it never got any easier. That anyone for any reason, particularly a child, should be homeless was a tragedy she could scarcely imagine, though she saw it nearly every day.

"More now than a few years ago," she said out loud. "People who never dreamed of being without jobs or food or homes are finding themselves in exactly that predicament. Oh, Father, thank You for allowing me to serve them in some small way!"

Pray for them.

The voice, though silent, was as familiar to her as her own heartbeat. She'd heard it for years and cherished it above life itself. "I do," she said. "And I will continue to, Lord, I promise."

She realized then that the words had been more than a general reminder; they were a specific command.

"For the little girl and her family?"

Yes. That was it. She knew it without doubt then, and she sensed God was calling her to more than a one-time "bless them" prayer.

"They're on my prayer list, Father," she said. "Daily. I promise."

The warmth of a divine smile filled the car as she turned onto the familiar street where the two-bedroom bungalow sat waiting for her. She'd changed little of the house or yard since John's death. They'd bought it together, thinking they would trade up as their family and income grew. Karen had long since come to realize that God had known all along that it would just be the two of them—Karen and her Lord—living there together, and the cozy cottage turned out to be just the right size.

By the time she pulled into the driveway and walked the few steps to the front door, her weariness had dissipated. Instead of heading straight for bed, which she originally intended to do when she left the soup kitchen, she fixed herself a cup of decaf and sat down at the kitchen table, her Bible and journal open in front of her.

"Little girl who loves donuts—and her family," she wrote at the top of her prayer list. "Lord, I sure would like to know their names at some point, but I suppose it's enough that You already do. Thank You for bringing them into my life."

Bowing her head and closing her eyes, she began what she sensed would be a long commitment of intercession for the family who had just been added to her journal.

❄ ❄ ❄

Josie's back ached and her right arm tingled from having Susanna resting on it most of the night. By the time she opened her eyes and glanced around, people were milling about, gathering their belongings into sacks or backpacks, and, for the most part, speaking in hushed tones as others continued to sleep.

Susanna's straight blonde hair was splayed around her head like a halo, her mouth open as she breathed deeply. Josie smiled. *That girl can sleep anywhere—thank God. Since anywhere is pretty much where we end up sleeping these days.*

"I'm hungry, Mom."

Startled, Josie turned to find her son sitting up and rubbing his eyes. "When do you think those donuts will be ready?"

Josie chuckled. "Wasn't it just yesterday afternoon that you said you were so full you never wanted to eat again?"

Jacob's smile was sheepish. "That was yesterday. This is today, and I woke up thinking about donuts. I sure hope they have chocolate ones."

"Now, Jacob, you know we can't be picky. We'll just take whatever we can get, OK?" When he nodded and shrugged, she added, "And I heard fruit mentioned too—apples, I think—so let's be sure to get at least one of those. We need to eat as healthy as we can."

"I know, Mom." He grinned. "But I still hope they have chocolate donuts."

Chocolate or not, Josie was glad that at least they wouldn't start the morning with empty stomachs, as they had done far too often lately. That was no way for children to begin the day, and though she had a few dollars and a couple of food vouchers left to tide them over until her next check arrived, they had to use them wisely.

"Breakfast will be ready in ten minutes," came an announcement. "Please line up near the door with all your belongings, ready to leave once you receive your food. We will be closing up in half an hour."

"Wake up, sleepyhead," Josie called, touching her daughter's shoulder. "Time for breakfast."

25

Susanna's eyes flew open. "Donuts?" she asked, pulling herself to a sitting position.

Josie laughed. "Yes, sweetheart. Donuts. And apples too."

Susanna's grin spread across her face. "It's going to be a good day, isn't it, Mommy?"

Josie's laugh died in her chest. A good day? How long had it been since they'd actually had one of those? Did she dare hope they'd ever have another . . . or would she forever have to settle for defining a good day as one that included free donuts at a makeshift shelter?

"Sure," she said, determined not to put a damper on her child's enthusiasm. "I'm sure it will be a good day. Now, let's gather everything together so we'll be ready to go after we get our food. There are bathrooms we can use outside in the courtyard where we ate yesterday, but we'll have to wait in line. Get your jackets on. It's going to be cold out there."

CHAPTER 3

The winter sunshine of the day before now hid behind ominous clouds as the trio stepped outside into the cold, crowded courtyard. By the time they'd snaked their way through the line and used the restrooms, Josie had nearly forgotten the welcome warmth of the warehouse where they'd spent the night. The Pacific Northwest dampness was already seeping back into her bones, and she knew her children felt it by the way they tugged at the zippers on their jackets and donned their mittens without being reminded.

Silently they trudged out onto the street, leaving their most recent shelter behind as Josie wondered where she might take her children to keep them out of the weather. From the looks of the sky and the feel of the wind, rain would be upon them shortly.

The mall? No doubt the only major one in the little town of Riverview would be crowded with the day-after-Thanksgiving shoppers, searching for bargains as they checked off names from their shopping lists. After all, wasn't that what Josie had done just the year before? Though she'd had to fight the ache in her heart from no longer having her mother to accompany her on the annual outing, at least she'd enjoyed the familiarity of shopping for her husband and children, and even splurging on a couple of favorite items for herself.

Not this year, she told herself. *I'll be doing well to have enough money left from my December check to rent us a room on Christmas Eve.* The thought birthed a determination in her heart to set aside enough to do just that, even if it meant spending an extra night or two sleeping behind the cleaners beforehand. So long as the nights were dry, they could handle that. Even misty nights weren't too bad in that particular spot because they could huddle under the overhang of the building. But when the wind and rain kicked up too much, it was no better than sleeping in the middle of the street.

If only the library were open today, she mused, as the three of them crossed the street at a nearly deserted intersection. *We could at least spend a few hours there.*

She thought of her new friend Louise, the lady she'd become acquainted with over the last few weeks. Louise worked at the library during the week, and when she was there she made it a point to let Josie and the kids stay as long as the doors were open, despite the library's policy to the contrary, brought on by the growing number of homeless who tended to make it their daily hangout.

"Are we going to the mall, Mom?" Jacob asked, interrupting her reverie.

Josie glanced down at her son and smiled. "I imagine so," she said. "It's warm there, and it will be open late. It'll be a madhouse, with everyone trying to take advantage of the sales, but at least we can blend in a little easier that way. Maybe no one will ask us to leave."

A flash of pain darted through Jacob's brown eyes, but he nodded and turned away. At seven years old he had come to know class rejection, something that never even crossed his mind before his father died and life as he knew it disintegrated.

"Mommy?"

Susanna's tug on her sleeve caught Josie's attention. She turned her gaze down toward her daughter.

"Am I ever going to go to school like other kids?"

28

A jolt of heat pierced Josie's heart, and she nearly crumpled to the sidewalk. For almost a year Susanna had done nothing but talk about starting kindergarten, and judging by how much the then four-year-old had enjoyed the two mornings each week when she attended preschool, Josie had been certain her daughter would shine as a student. But by the time September rolled around, Josie hadn't even known what to list as their permanent address. As a result, Susanna had yet to attend even one day of kindergarten.

I should have listened to that social worker's advice and tried to move to a larger city with more facilities for the homeless. Maybe I could at least have found a way to keep my kids in school.

Tears burned her eyes as she forced herself to speak. "Of course you are, sweetheart, and so will Jacob. We just need to be a little patient until we get settled somewhere."

The doubt in her daughter's eyes was evident, but she nodded as if accepting Josie's words. Still, it wasn't as hard with Susanna, since she was only five and could easily wait another year to start school. Surely they'd have a home by then . . . wouldn't they?

But it was Jacob that worried her most. She knew he desperately wanted to return to school and play with his friends again, but she also knew she couldn't send him in dirty, tattered clothes, especially when she didn't even know where they would sleep each night. So far she'd been able to keep him reading on a fairly regular basis, but she knew that wasn't enough. In fact, she was concerned she could be in trouble legally if she didn't find a way to resolve the issue soon.

One thing at a time, she told herself. *A warm place to spend the day . . . at the mall. Check. The apples from the shelter for lunch. Check. Dinner and a place to sleep tonight? Still up in the air.*

The entrance to the mall was in sight now, and she anticipated the welcome blast of warm air when they walked inside, more for her children than for herself. If they could find a quiet spot to eat their apples later, it would be a decent start to their day.

"Mommy?"

Susanna again. Josie prayed it wasn't another question about school. She kept her eyes fixed on the mall as they continued to walk toward it.

"We forgot to say good-bye to the nice man."

Josie frowned and looked down at Susanna. The nice man?

"Rick," Jacob said. "His name is Rick. He's a Vietnam vet."

Josie's eyes widened. Susanna was right. They had left the shelter that morning without even thanking him for bringing them there the night before.

"I'm sorry," she said. "You're right. We should have said good-bye to him. But I'm sure he understands."

"Maybe we'll see him again," Susanna suggested, the hint of a smile lighting her upturned face.

Josie nodded. "Maybe. Now let's get inside that mall and warm up, shall we?"

They'd arrived at the entrance, and Jacob opened the door and held it as Josie and Susanna—and a handful of other shoppers—made their way inside. Though Josie had anticipated a crowd, she'd had no idea it would be so bad.

"Hold my hands tight," she commanded. "Nobody goes anywhere on their own. We stick together, no matter what. Got it?"

Both children nodded, and then the three of them set out to make their way through the crush of humanity.

❄ ❄ ❄

The mouthwatering smells of hot pretzels and gooey cinnamon rolls had Josie's stomach growling in minutes. No doubt her children felt the same way, but they all knew the only lunch they'd have this day were the apples stowed in Jacob's backpack. Josie knew she should be grateful to have them, but they were a pitiful substitute for the meal she'd like to provide for her family. Maybe something would turn up for dinner so she wouldn't have to dip into what little money or food vouchers she had left.

They worked their way, sometimes inches at a time, through the wall of constantly moving shoppers. Some walked with them, others against them, all jostling and rushing and streaming toward another bargain, another . Would the future recipients of those purchases truly appreciate them once they were received? Not for long, Josie imagined, judging by past experience when she too had taken such things for granted.

She spotted an elderly couple helping one another up from a bench just a few feet away, and Josie pushed toward the welcome spot. The two seniors smiled at her as she slipped into their newly vacated seats, pulling her children down with her, one on each side, as they filled the bench. This was perfect—not really private, but at least out of the middle of the migrating throngs. It was still a bit early for lunch, but perhaps they could sit there awhile and just read or talk or people-watch before biting into their waiting apples.

"Mommy, I'm hungry."

Susanna's statement came sooner than Josie had expected. She glanced at her watch, one of only two pieces of jewelry she'd managed to keep after Sam died. The other was her wedding ring, and she'd thought often of selling both of them but hadn't been able to bring herself to do so. Besides, the watch was the only way they had of being on time anywhere, including appointments at social services offices where missing an appointment could mean missing a monthly check.

"It's not even eleven yet," she told Susanna. "We should wait a little longer before we eat."

Susanna's lip quivered as she nodded. "OK, Mommy." She turned her head to the front, and Josie wondered what was running through the little girl's mind. *I'm glad I don't know,* she told herself. *My heart can't take much more.*

"Do you hear that song, Mom?"

Jacob's question interrupted her thoughts, and she turned to look at her son's upturned face. He wasn't smiling.

She frowned, straining to focus. What song? She listened. Had Christmas carols been playing all along? Apparently so, because now that Jacob had brought it to her attention, she heard it quite clearly—the familiar song proclaiming that the singer would be home for Christmas, even if only in his dreams.

The implications were staggering. She didn't have to ask why her seven-year-old had chosen to point out that particular song. But what did he want from her? How did she respond to such an observation? The chances that they would be home anywhere for Christmas—unless she was somehow able to save enough money from her December check to rent a room on Christmas Eve—were slim to none.

"Mrs. Meyers? Is that you?"

The somewhat familiar voice felt like an intrusion. It obviously belonged to someone younger than Josie but older than her children. How she hated running into people she'd known . . . before. Especially at this particular moment, which for some reason made her feel especially exposed and vulnerable. But so long as she remained in this relatively small town, what else could she expect?

She raised her head and locked gazes with a young woman whose short, two-tone blonde hair looked as if it had exploded out of her head. Diamond studs glistened in her earlobes and nose. The tattoo of a butterfly decorated the right side of her neck. A black pullover sweater, tight designer jeans, and black high-heeled boots completed her stunning appearance. Josie imagined she was pretty in a gaudy sort of way, but it was the teenager's dark, sparkling eyes that made her attractive.

Margaret? Marie? Megan? She ran through the names in her memory bank, sure the girl's name began with an *m*, but not sure why she thought that. Where had they met? How did they know one another?

"Melody!" Jacob jumped up from the bench as the young woman opened her arms and pulled him into an embrace.

"Hi, Jacob," she said, gazing down at him with a wide grin. "How are you? I've missed you!"

"I've missed you too," he said. "A lot!"

Melody. Josie remembered then. The teen babysat for the family down the street, the one whose son, Nate, was only a year or so younger than Jacob. Once or twice Jacob had visited there when Melody was watching Nate and his younger brother. Jacob had come home raving about how much fun Nate's babysitter was. And, of course, Josie had made it a point to meet Melody and to check with Nate's parents before agreeing to allow Jacob to stay there when she was babysitting.

Josie smiled, pleased to see Jacob so happy but embarrassed at how they must appear to this young woman. She dreaded the questions that were sure to follow.

"How are you?" Melody asked. "I haven't seen you in ages." Her smile faded then, as an obvious memory flitted through her dark eyes. "Oh, I'm sorry," she said, focusing on Josie. "I just remembered the last time I was babysitting for Nate, and his mom told me your husband died. I'm really, really sorry."

Josie nodded, trying to swallow the familiar lump that had popped up in her throat. "Thank you," she managed to say, then determined to change the subject. "So what are you doing now? You're not babysitting anymore?"

Melody's posture relaxed as they moved on to a more comfortable topic. "No, I graduated high school in June, and now

I'm working part-time and going to the junior college. I'm not sure what I want to get into yet, so I'm just taking some general subjects for now."

Josie smiled and added a touch of enthusiasm to her voice. "That's wonderful," she said. "So are you still living at home with your parents?"

Melody nodded. "Yeah. It seemed the smartest thing to do for now. It's just too expensive to move out on my own yet."

Josie swallowed the lump before it could return. She knew only too well how difficult it was to get established in a house or apartment . . . or any sort of living situation, for that matter. The girl was smart to stay home while she could.

"We don't have a home," Susanna said.

Josie gasped, as she felt her eyes widen. Heat crept up into her face, and she fought the tears that pricked her eyes. The last thing she'd wanted was to announce their homeless condition to an eighteen- or nineteen-year-old who would no doubt pity them but also be embarrassed at the news.

"Susanna," Jacob said, "you're not supposed to tell people that."

Susanna's head drooped, along with her shoulders. Josie reached out and put her arm around her, drawing the girl close. "It's OK, sweetheart."

"But, Mom, you said—"

Josie glanced at Jacob. "I know, son."

"You . . . you're homeless?"

Melody's words came more as a question than a statement, and they sliced through Josie's armor, straight to her already raw heart. Humiliated in front of a girl who wasn't even an adult yet! How many people would she tell? Oh, why had Josie brought her children here on such a busy day? Why hadn't she realized they were bound to run into someone they knew? But it had been the only warm place she could think of. The only place . . .

She felt Melody's hand on her shoulder then, and reluctantly she lifted her head, only to find the young woman staring down at her, tears pooling in her dark eyes. "I had no idea," she said. "I didn't know."

Nor did I want you to, Josie thought, but she bit her lip. The girl was being kind; there was no need to snap at her.

"Come home with me tonight," she said. "Please. My parents would want you to. They'd be upset with me if I didn't invite you, knowing you have no place else to go."

Josie shook her head. "No. No, we couldn't possibly do that. Really, we're all right. We have somewhere to go tonight. Please, don't worry about us. We're fine."

"No, we're not, Mommy," Susanna said. "We only have apples for lunch, and I'm hungry. And I don't want to sleep behind the cleaners again."

"That's it," Melody said, pulling a cell phone from her pocket and punching a number. "I'm calling home to tell them you're coming with me."

Trembling, Josie reached toward the phone to pull it away before Melody could make the call, but it was too late. In less than a moment it was settled; they would stay overnight at Melody's home. "Mom said you can use my brother Todd's room. He's visiting a friend for the weekend. Come on. Let's go. I've done enough shopping for one day anyway. This place is a madhouse."

Susanna jumped to her feet and began to tug on Josie's hand. "Come on, Mommy. Please. Let's go to Melody's house. Please, Mommy."

Josie hesitated, glancing again at Jacob, who nodded his agreement. "Just for tonight, Mom. Please?"

She sighed and stood to her feet. Just when she thought she had no more pride to lose, something like this happened and she found out otherwise. Still fighting tears, she allowed her

35

daughter to pull her along, while Jacob walked and chatted with Melody directly in front of them.

One night, Josie told herself. *One night in a warm house and maybe even a meal or two. But that's it. Then we leave, period. We can't take advantage of people. We just can't.*

By the time they maneuvered back through the crowded mall and outside into the cold, Josie had resigned herself to further humiliation in return for a good night's sleep for her children. Tomorrow would come soon enough, and they'd be back on the streets once again.

※ ※ ※

The three-bedroom home in the old area of town was much smaller than the one Josie had lived in when Sam was alive, but it was warm and safe . . . and Melody's parents had insisted they plan on staying until Sunday when their son was due home. That meant two nights in the same place, and it sounded like the next best thing to heaven at this point, at least so far as Josie was concerned.

After a light meal of leftovers from their Thanksgiving feast the day before, Mrs. Lund—who insisted Josie call her Arlene—had sat and visited with Josie while Melody entertained the children and Mr. Lund tinkered in his garage. The hint at normalcy was almost more than Josie could bear, but she liked Arlene and expressed her appreciation to the point that the middle-aged woman nearly begged her to stop.

"Please," she said, holding up her hand as they sat across from one another at the kitchen table, "you really don't have to thank me. I know you appreciate it, and I just wish we could do more." She shook her head. "I don't see how it's possible there isn't somewhere for a family like yours to go—somewhere permanent, I mean. Soup kitchens are fine and shelters are wonderful, but I had no idea how temporary they were. I don't know how I could have been so naïve. Our church has a food pantry, but it's only open twice a week. That's not nearly enough, is it?"

Josie fought tears as she answered. "It's not, but . . . we appreciate it anyway. There are several around town, and we try to get to them whenever possible—and when they're open. They supplement what we can get with our food vouchers. I . . . I try to save the money we get at the first of each month for shelter when the weather's at its worst."

Tears had formed in Arlene's gray eyes, and Josie remembered thinking the woman looked older than her forty-three years. But then sadness could do that to people, even if the sadness belonged to someone else.

Now Josie lay in sixteen-year-old Todd Lund's single bed, with Susanna tucked in beside her. Jacob had sprawled happily on a quilt on the floor next to the closet. The arrangement didn't leave for much walking space in the small room, but Josie had rejoiced to see how quickly both children had fallen asleep in their temporary quarters.

One more night here, she thought. *That's one night more of security than we usually have, but then we have to move on. It'll still be a few days before I get another check. Where will we sleep until then?*

The memory of her mother's words echoed in her heart, as if in answer to her question: *God knows. The Bible says He owns the cattle on a thousand hills. He can certainly provide a place for you to sleep . . . if you'll just ask Him.*

Her mind rebelled at the thought. Ask a favor from the God who had betrayed them, deserted them, nearly destroyed them? Why should she?

Susanna moaned in her sleep, and Josie had her answer. She needed to pray for her children's sake. If it were just her, she'd sleep on the street in the rain every night for the rest of her life before she'd grovel at the feet of an uncaring Deity—particularly One who seemed to delight in ignoring her requests. But it wasn't just her. There were two innocent children with needs she simply couldn't meet on her own. As much as she hated to admit it, prayer seemed to be her only option.

She squeezed her eyes shut, swallowed her doubt and irritation, and began to present her requests to a faraway God.

CHAPTER 4

Saturday passed in a warm haze, with the children sleeping in and whooping with delight over pancakes for breakfast. But by Saturday night Josie was having a difficult time maintaining any semblance of joy. It had been raining nearly nonstop for the past twenty-four hours and showed no signs of letting up any time soon. *Not before May or June,* Josie thought, terrified once again at the prospect of spending a long winter on the streets with her children.

But what else can we do? There's no family, no friends, no one who will take us in for more than a night or two. The Lunds have been great, but I know what's going to happen tomorrow. First they'll want us to go to church with them, and then after we come home for lunch, they'll send us packing before Todd gets home. Then what?

She shook her head, staring into the darkness as she listened to her children's steady breathing. How could they sleep so peacefully when they had no idea where they'd lay their heads the next night? Oh, to be a child again, with no care beyond the moment!

That's not true, she reminded herself. *Not anymore. Once my children had the security of two parents who loved them, a nice home, food on the table, toys and television . . . all the things normal people have. Now what? They've enjoyed two nights in a borrowed bedroom, then back to reality tomorrow.*

She clenched her jaw. *I know one thing for sure. As kind as the Lunds have been, I'm not going to let them talk us into going to church with them tomorrow. I'll get the kids up early and we'll be ready to set out right after breakfast. Sure, it'll be cold and wet out there, but it isn't going to be any better a few hours later. And since it's obvious God hasn't made any attempt to answer my prayers for somewhere to go, we'll just skip the hypocrisy of attending church. I'd rather go back to the mall and sit on the bench where Melody found us on Friday.*

A tear slipped from her eye and trickled down her cheek, annoying her as it landed in her ear. She brushed it away, trying to ignore the disappointment that teased her as she considered how different things could have been all along the way if only God would answer her prayers once in a while.

All those years in church and Sunday school as a kid, she thought. *What a waste! Look where it got me. . . .*

Once again she heard her mother's voice, this time from the past, cautioning her to marry a Christian man and establish a Christian home. Josie knew her mother had cared for Sam, but she also knew he wasn't what anyone would consider a strong Christian. Sure, he'd gone to church with them on occasion, and almost always at Christmas and Easter, but Josie knew her mother had wanted so much more for her.

I trusted you, Sam, Josie thought, squeezing her eyes shut against the pain. *You said you'd take care of us. How could you have let things get so bad? Why didn't you tell me, prepare me somehow? How could you leave us, knowing what would happen when the little bit of money we had left ran out?*

A sob broke forth from her chest then, and she rolled onto her stomach and buried her face in the pillow. The last thing she wanted was for her children to hear her crying and realize how hopeless their situation truly was.

❄ ❄ ❄

Karen woke before daybreak, as she often did on Sundays. She spent time alone with the Lord each morning throughout the week, but Sundays were special. How she looked forward to this time of corporate worship, of coming together with her "forever family" to pray and sing and hear the pastor teach from the Bible. She also loved instructing the children in her five-year-old Sunday school class, as she'd done for so many years. Because she'd lost John so soon after their marriage and had chosen not to remarry, she'd also missed out on having children of her own, but the little ones in her class had filled that void nicely.

This morning, however, as she sat in her favorite armchair beside the window in the living room, her Bible resting in her lap, she once again remembered her commitment to pray for the woman with the two children. Scarcely a day went by that she didn't pray for many of the homeless people she served at the soup kitchen, but God had laid this little family on her heart for a specific purpose. Though she had yet to identify it, her Lord knew, and that was all that mattered.

Smiling, she closed her eyes and leaned her head back. "Father," she whispered. "Abba, Father."

The endearing and very personal term that she often used when speaking to God brought a familiar sense of warmth and peace to her heart, as she pictured the woman and her children and wondered where they might be this cool, gray morning. "You know where they are, Father," she said, "and what they need. Show me how to pray."

As she waited for her answer, she rested in the knowledge that it would certainly come. It always had before, though not necessarily in the way or at the time she anticipated. But that was all right. She trusted that her Father knew what was best, not only for her but for everyone on her prayer list as well. That

41

knowledge enabled her to pray in confidence, as she would do again this day.

And then she would climb into her car and drive to church to see the people she loved and to worship the God she adored. It would be the perfect ending to a very blessed Thanksgiving weekend.

※　※　※

A knock on the bedroom door startled Josie from a dream-filled sleep, though the clarity of her dream evaporated into vague images and colors as she jerked upright in the bed.

Where was she? The muted light in the room told her that morning had just begun to dawn. But even as her thoughts gelled and she realized she and her children were sleeping in the Lunds' home, she wondered why someone would be knocking so early.

They probably want to remind us about being up and ready for church this morning, she thought, berating herself for not waking up earlier as she'd planned. Now she would have to face them and decline to accompany them to the service, even as she thanked them for their kindness in opening their home for the past two nights.

The knock came again. "Mrs. Meyers? Josie? Are you awake? I need to speak with you, please."

The voice belonged to Arlene. Josie sighed and threw back the covers, careful not to disturb her still sleeping children. Padding quietly across the small room and stepping over Jacob in the process, she cracked the door and peeked out.

"Give me just a minute," she whispered.

Arlene smiled and nodded before turning away.

Josie picked up the chenille robe Arlene had loaned her and threw it over her shoulders before sliding her feet into the borrowed slippers that waited beside the bed. She steeled herself against the pain of knowing they would be leaving this warm refuge in a matter of hours, dumped back on the street to wander and try to survive until her check arrived at the post office.

She closed the door softly behind her and made a beeline for the bathroom in the hallway, staying only as long as necessary before slipping back out into the hall and making her way toward the kitchen where the light shone and the aroma of freshly brewed coffee beckoned. Oh, how the comforts she once took for granted now seemed luxuries just out of her reach!

Arlene sat at the table, a mug of steaming coffee in front of her. She too was wrapped in a robe and slippers, her short brown hair only slightly out of place but her lack of makeup evident. She smiled in welcome.

"Help yourself to coffee," she said. "I'll fix some eggs and toast as soon as Jerry and Melody join us."

Josie knew her smile was thin, but it was the best she could muster. She made her way to the counter and filled one of the mugs that sat beside the coffeepot. Had it really been only a few months since she'd made coffee in her own kitchen, pouring flavored creamer from the refrigerator into the hot, dark liquid as she planned her day? Now she was more than content to drink her coffee black, savoring every sip.

She sat down across from Arlene, waiting for the inevitable invitation to church and then the apology that would follow as she explained to Josie that she and her children would have to leave by the end of the day. At least it was Sunday, and by tomorrow she would be able to take her children to the library for most of the day since Louise would be working.

Arlene cleared her throat, and Josie braced herself, trying to formulate her excuse for declining the forthcoming invitation to church.

"I imagine you already know that Jerry and I will be going to church this morning—Melody, too, of course."

Josie nodded, but before she could say anything, Arlene continued.

"You and the children are welcome to join us if you'd like. I know it's not the church you usually attend, but we'd be happy to take you along." Arlene smiled. "It's entirely up to you, but I just wanted to make the offer. If you'd rather catch a bus or something to your own church, or just stay here and rest, that's fine too. Whatever you prefer."

Josie raised her eyebrows. She hadn't expected such options, but she gladly accepted them. "Thank you," she said, ignoring the woman's misconception that they regularly attended church somewhere else. "We may just do that — stay here for a while, I mean. That is, if you're sure you don't mind . . . ."

Arlene's smile widened. "Of course we don't mind. You're more than welcome." She paused before continuing. "In fact, Jerry and I have been talking, and we wondered if you might like to . . . well, I mean, if you don't mind sleeping on the sofa in the living room, we thought you might . . . want to stay awhile longer."

Josie's heart rate kicked into overdrive, and she slopped a drop of hot coffee on her hand as she plopped the mug down on the table. "Stay . . . longer?" she repeated, wondering if she'd heard her correctly. "You mean, you'd let us . . . stay here with you, in your home . . . for a little while?"

Arlene reached across the table and covered Josie's hand with her own. Her skin was smooth and warm and nearly brought tears to Josie's eyes. "We can't possibly put you and your children out in the rain," she said. "I don't know how long we can have you here, since this is a rental and our landlord has always been adamant about no permanent houseguests, only visitors. But we can try it for a week or two and see what happens. Maybe longer. Who knows?"

Josie nearly choked on the familiar lump in her throat, as she brushed away the tears that spilled from her eyes. "I . . . I don't know what to say." Her shoulders shook, and she felt herself dangerously near meltdown. She took a deep breath. "I don't want to cause you any trouble with your landlord."

"We'll deal with that issue if we come to it," Arlene said, her smile back in place. "But Jerry and Melody and I—and Todd, too, since we called and talked to him about it—all agree that we want to at least give it a try. You mentioned that you couldn't even get your kids into school without a permanent address, so maybe this will help. And I have a friend who homeschools her kids, so she might have some suggestions for you too."

Josie's control disintegrated, and she buried her face in her hands, her stomach clenching from the intensity of her sobs. In moments she felt Arlene scoot her chair beside her and pull her into her arms. Josie knew the woman wasn't quite old enough to be her mother, but she couldn't help thinking of her mom as she cried on her new friend's shoulder.

CHAPTER 5

Josie still struggled to absorb the events of the morning. After finally drying her tears, she'd gone back to the bedroom to share the news with her children. They were still sleeping, so she'd showered and dressed before waking them for breakfast.

"I have some good news for you," she'd announced once she was certain they were both alert enough to understand what she was about to tell them. "The Lunds have offered to let us stay here awhile longer—not in this room, of course, because Todd is coming home this afternoon. But they said we can sleep on the sofa bed in the living room. Isn't that wonderful?"

"Yes!" Susanna's response was immediate as she jumped up and began bouncing on the bed. "Yes, yes, yes! We're going to live here with the Lunds!"

"I didn't say that," Josie cautioned, snagging her daughter in midair and reminding her not to jump on the furniture. "I said we're going to stay here *awhile*. We don't really know how long that might be, but at least for now we have a safe place to spend our nights."

"Does that mean I can go back to school?" Jacob, ever the practical one in the family, brought a smile to Josie's lips.

"Maybe," she said. "We'll see. Though I might check into homeschooling, just in case we aren't able to stay here for very long."

"What about me?" Susanna asked. "Can I go to school now too—finally?"

Josie felt her smile wilt. "We'll see. But just like Jacob, if you can't go to school, I'll get some studies for you and we'll work on them ourselves."

"And when we don't have a home anymore?" Susanna asked. "When we have to move out of here, what then?"

Josie sighed. There were no easy answers to her children's questions.

"We'll deal with that when we come to it," she said. "Now I want you two to get dressed and come to the kitchen for breakfast. Mrs. Lund is fixing eggs and toast, and we don't want to keep her waiting."

Susanna scrambled from bed and grabbed her clothes. "I get dibs on the bathroom," she announced, scurrying to the door.

"Don't forget, I need in there too," Jacob called after her.

Susanna didn't answer. She might be only five years old, but since she was a toddler she'd had an aversion to dirt. She wanted to be clean and neat at all times, a virtual impossibility when living on the streets. No wonder she wanted to squeal with delight and jump on the bed at the good news that they could stay here with the Lunds for a while. Josie just hoped it would be long enough to enable her to find a viable alternative before their time here ran out.

❄ ❄ ❄

They'd scarcely finished breakfast when Josie found herself caught up in the flurry to leave for church. More than once she opened her mouth to offer an excuse to stay behind, particularly since Arlene had opened that door for her. But the look of excitement on her children's faces, coupled with the Lunds' generosity and hospitality, dried up the words before they could get past her throat. On Saturday Arlene had graciously allowed her to wash the few clothes she and her children had, so she couldn't even beg off due to not having anything presentable to wear.

And then they were in the car, Josie squeezed into the backseat with Jacob and Susanna, with Mr. and Mrs. Lund in the front. Melody had caught an earlier ride with her friends so they could attend the college-age class, saying she would meet everyone in the sanctuary in time for the service. Arlene had even given Josie an extra Bible to carry with her.

She fingered the worn leather as she stared out the window, ignoring the chatter beside her. *It's a study in contrasts,* she thought. *My children are the sunshine crew, and I'm as dark and dreary as the gray Washington sky.*

I should be grateful, she reminded herself. *After all, I did pray last night, and now we have a place to stay for a few days . . . maybe even weeks. But it could be a coincidence. It's not like God's answered my prayers before. Why would He suddenly start now?*

"Mommy?"

Josie jerked her gaze from the window and turned to look down at Susanna, who was pulling on her sleeve. "Mommy, did you hear what Mrs. Lund said about caroling? I want to go."

Josie blinked. She most certainly had not heard what Arlene said. Her mind, as usual, had been lost in her own dark thoughts. She wasn't proud of that fact but seemed unable to escape it these days.

She cleared her throat. "I'm sorry. No, I didn't."

Arlene turned in her seat to look back at Josie, who sat directly behind her. "I was just telling the children about the sleigh ride we're planning in a couple of weeks. We'll all bundle up and pile into the back of a truck—not really a sleigh, of course, but we just call it that—and we'll go through town singing Christmas carols. After that we'll head back to the church for hot chocolate and cookies. We'd love it if you all would join us."

Josie's heart lurched at the memory of many such outings as a child, with both parents before her father died and then later with her mother. Those had been joyous times, full of love and security . . . and faith. Yes, she had believed . . . once. But all that was behind her now, lost with her loved ones and the house she'd once called home.

She blinked and pulled herself back to the present. How could she say no to one of the few happy opportunities her children had in their current lives? She smiled. "Of course," she said. "We'd love to. Thanks."

Susanna squealed and clapped her hands. Even Jacob beamed as he leaned back against the seat. If only Josie could be sure they wouldn't be back sleeping behind the cleaners by the time the carolers climbed into the back of the truck, she might be able to relax and anticipate the outing herself.

❄ ❄ ❄

It had been an especially tough night for Rick, as he'd been unable to get into any of the shelters. Families with children got priority, which he totally agreed they should, and though he got second priority as a senior citizen, he wasn't elderly enough that he felt justified in taking a spot from an older person or even a woman without children, so he always gave up his spot for one of them. As a result he spent more nights on the street than inside.

His tiny disability stipend from the military and his even smaller Social Security check would arrive in a few days. Until then he'd just have to make due. He'd been on the streets long enough that he knew where to find at least one meal nearly every day, and he was usually able to snag a semi-dry spot to sleep. The last couple of nights he'd been huddling down in the spot behind the cleaners where he'd found the woman with her two children on Thanksgiving night. He was almost relieved not to find them there lately, hoping that meant they'd found some sort of shelter for the time being. Of course, he knew that even women with children sometimes had to sleep outside, simply because there weren't enough shelters with available beds. It saddened him to think of those sweet kids out on the street somewhere.

Coughing into his handkerchief, he shivered as he pulled his jacket tighter and pushed toward the church. Regardless of how he felt or what the weather was like, he always made sure he got to church on Sunday mornings. He could see it now, just down the block, and he smiled despite the ever-increasing fire in his chest. There was nothing like stepping inside the house of God to dispel all fears and doubts, aches and pains, and even the occasional depression and anxiety that had haunted him for decades. He knew the feelings were caused by the mental disorder he'd been diagnosed with after he returned from 'Nam, but it was still a battle when the dark thoughts loomed.

The parking lot was nearly full when Rick arrived, and the front doors were already closed when he mounted the steps. He liked it that way, purposely showing up just a few minutes late so he could slip in quietly and sit in the back. Though a few of the ushers and a handful of parishioners sometimes nodded in recognition when he entered, most didn't even notice him as they were already on their feet and singing.

"Blessed assurance," the congregation sang, "Jesus is mine."

Rick's heart swelled. He didn't have much in this world that he could claim as his own, but Jesus was surely his—his Savior, his Lord, his best Friend. He was the One who had gotten him through the horrors of Vietnam, the pain and fears that accompanied his months of hospitalization after he was caught in the crossfire of an ambush, and the numbing realization that though his physical wounds had finally healed, his mind never would—not completely. Family and friends eventually pulled away from him, jobs eluded him, and relationships terrified him.

The streets soon became his refuge, made bearable because Jesus accompanied him there.

"Thank You, Lord," he whispered, as the congregation continued to sing. "Thank You that You never leave me or forsake me. You're the only reason I'm still breathing today. I just wish I knew why You have me here, why You haven't just taken me home to be with You. What good am I, Jesus? What purpose could I possibly have?"

You are My hands and My feet, came the quiet answer to his heart. *You speak My words and bless others in My name.*

Tears stung his eyes. "How?" he whispered. "I'm no good to anyone. I want to help, but I don't know how."

Your want-to is all I need, son. I will use you to fulfill My purposes.

Son. Each time Rick heard the heavenly whisper of that word, his heart warmed and his spirit soared. It no longer mattered that he had no home, no family, no earthly belongings or profitable future. He had a home in heaven, an eternity with the One he loved above all else. And ultimately, he knew, that was all anyone really needed anyway.

CHAPTER 6

As always, Sunday service came to a close much too quickly to suit Karen. If it were up to her, she'd stay there all day, right through to the evening gathering. She imagined that was because, unlike most people in the congregation, she didn't have a family waiting for her to go home and cook Sunday dinner.

She smiled to herself as people began to move toward the aisles and the level of conversation rose around her, muting the background praise music coming from the worship team behind the pulpit. At least their church still had a Sunday evening service, and for that she was grateful. She understood the practice was becoming a rarity these days, and she couldn't imagine not returning to church after a pleasant and restful Sunday afternoon.

As she stepped out into the aisle, she caught a tentative smile from a small blonde girl. The child looked familiar, but Karen struggled to remember her name.

"You're the nice lady who let us in to sleep at the warehouse," the girl announced, her blue eyes alight with recognition.

Karen raised her eyebrows. The warehouse? Of course! That's where she'd seen the child before, on Thanksgiving night. This was the family she'd just put on her prayer list! She raised her gaze from the girl to the slightly older boy standing beside her and the thin, fair-haired woman holding on to both of them. The woman's cheeks were flushed, and she dropped her eyes the instant Karen looked into them.

She knew the look. Working in homeless shelters, that embarrassed expression, the humiliated stance, was all too familiar.

"Well, hello to all of you," Karen said, her voice a bit more cheerful than usual. "It's wonderful to see you here. How are you?"

The mother raised her head and opened her mouth as if to answer, but the little girl beat her to it. "We came with our friends," she said. "We live with them now."

"Oh no, that's not true," the child's mother said quickly, her cheeks turning a darker shade of red. "We're just . . . staying with them for a few days."

Karen smiled, praying she could put them all at ease. "Why, that's wonderful," she said. "I love visiting friends. And I'm so glad they've brought you here to our church."

54   The little knot they'd formed during their brief conversation was obviously holding up the line headed for the exit, so Karen stepped back into the pew, hoping the little family would follow. Instead, the woman quickly excused herself and explained that their hosts were waiting for them.

"It was nice to see you again," she said, her thin-lipped smile appearing forced.

Karen nodded. "Yes, it was. And I do hope it won't be the last time. My name is Karen, by the way."

"I'm Susanna," the girl announced, her eyes dancing as she pointed toward her brother and then mother. "And that's my brother, Jacob, and my mom. Her name is Josephine, but everybody just calls her Josie."

The woman named Josie was already nudging her children toward the back door, even as Susanna looked back and made her introductions. Karen laughed and waved. "Well, thank you very much, Susanna. I hope to see you again soon!"

Susanna waved, as the three of them moved on. Karen returned the gesture and then joined the stragglers and followed after them. By the time she stepped outside, Josie and her children were walking toward the parking lot with the Lunds, longtime friends of Karen's.

That's just like Jerry and Arlene, she thought. *They've never had much in the way of material goods, but they never hesitate to share whatever they can and help others in need. I'm so glad they've connected with Josie and her kids. Thank You, Lord. I know that was a divine appointment on Your part, and I will continue to pray for them.*

By the time she too had reached the parking lot and climbed inside her car, her stomach was growling and she realized she'd be ready for some of that stew she'd left bubbling in the Crock-Pot at home. She carefully maneuvered out of her space and past the parishioners toward the driveway, then exited onto the street. In the distance she spotted the Vietnam vet named Rick, whom she'd come to know during her many years at the shelter. No doubt he would enjoy a home-cooked meal, and she'd enjoy the company. Dismissing what she knew would be well-meaning advice from others if they knew what she was contemplating, she pulled up beside Rick and hit the window button. It slid down as he turned and smiled in recognition.

"How about joining me for lunch?" she said. "I've got more than I can eat, just waiting for me at home."

Rick's hesitation didn't last long. In less than a minute he was buckled up in the passenger seat of Karen's car, thanking her profusely for the offer and struggling to hold back his familiar cough. Karen knew he wasn't well, and there wasn't much she could do about that. But she could at least offer him a warm meal and some pleasant conversation. Besides, it wouldn't be the first time. She and Rick had shared a dozen or so meals over the years, and she was pleased to have the opportunity to do so once again.

55

❄ ❄ ❄

Josie woke up to the aroma of coffee on Monday morning, and her first reaction was amazement that she and her children were sleeping in a house and that they might be able to stay there for an indefinite period of time. Sitting up on the side of the sofa bed, she slid her feet into slippers, picked up the robe at the end of the bed, and left the children sleeping while she grabbed some clothes and headed for the bathroom in the hall. She was determined to get an early start, heading first to talk to the lady Arlene had told her about who knew the ins and outs of homeschooling. That seemed the best option to Josie, as their living situation was still tenuous at best. No sense getting the kids enrolled in school, only to have to pull them out a week or so later.

I don't want to take advantage of the Lunds, she thought, turning on the shower and stepping out of her robe and nightgown while she waited for the water to warm up. *The last thing they need is the three of us underfoot every day. Just having a safe place to sleep is enough. We can straighten up their living room and then go to the library for the day. If I can get the kids started with homeschooling, that would be the obvious place for them to do their studies anyway.*

She sighed as she stepped into the shower, letting the hot water wash away what still felt like weeks and months of dirt and grime. Sometimes she wondered if she'd ever feel clean again. But at least for now they had access to regular showers and clean clothes. Arlene had even mentioned that the church had a clothes closet where they could pick up some extra things sometime that week. It was hard for Josie to believe she could get excited about hand-me-down clothes, but the truth was that Jacob and Susanna were outgrowing the only two outfits they each had, and Josie had been wondering how she would get them something that fit.

Luxuriating at the feel of sudsy shampoo in her straight, almost shoulder-length hair, the not-quite-thirty-year-old mom wondered at what exact point it had been that she crossed over from feeling like a young woman to an old hag. Losing her mother had taken its toll, and when Sam died she thought her heart and youth had died with him. Then she'd learned the extent of their financial situation and soon after found herself and her children on the outside of their home, looking from the sidewalk at their locked front door and asking themselves how such a tragedy had happened.

Where would they go? What would they do? Surely someone would help them!

Social agencies had tried. They'd given her food vouchers and emergency funds, helped her fill out endless paperwork to find permanent housing, even as they told her the waiting list was months long at best. Josie had hesitated to approach the church, since their attendance had been sporadic at best. But she finally did, and the pastor found them an occasional night's shelter here and there and even offered a few dollars for food. When that ran out, Josie had been too embarrassed to return and beg for more. Now, as weeks turned to months, they were still technically homeless, even though they currently had a roof over their heads for the time being.

"I can't let myself think about that," she whispered through clenched teeth. "We're here for now, and maybe we'll be able to stay until the weather gets better in the spring — maybe even long enough for me to save a little money or for us to get approved for housing. Oh God, please let that happen!"

The realization that she had just prayed out loud pierced her heart, and she hardened it against the onslaught. *Just because I prayed for a place to stay and now we're here with the Lunds doesn't mean I've forgiven You or believe in You again, because if You really loved me, You'd have answered my prayers long ago and we wouldn't be in this mess!*

Sticking her head under the nozzle, she let the spray wash away the shampoo from her hair as she forced her mind to focus on the task at hand. She had children to care for, and the first thing she had to do was find out about homeschooling them. If she could accomplish that by this evening, it would have been a successful day indeed.

❄ ❄ ❄

By early afternoon Josie and the children were comfortably settled in at the library. Josie had been pleased to discover that Washington State law did not require her to have her children registered in school until they were eight years old, so she had until spring to work things out for Jacob. Meanwhile, Arlene's friend had given her some used schoolbooks to help keep Jacob on track for his age group and even a couple of simple books to make Susanna feel included. It wasn't official homeschooling yet, but it afforded Josie time to either get that going or find a way to register Jacob and make sure he was able to attend school regularly.

Sensing someone nearby, Josie raised her eyes from the pamphlets she'd been studying about homeschooling requirements in Washington. Sure enough, her new friend Louise stood in front of the table where Josie and the kids sat. She smiled as she gazed down at them.

"Hey," she said, her angular face softened by a warm smile, "I've been wondering how you were doing. I missed you while we were closed over the Thanksgiving holiday."

Josie returned the smile, but before she could respond, Susanna, her face beaming, chimed in. "We ate turkey at the soup kitchen and slept there overnight. Then we went to the mall and saw Melody, and now we live with her."

Louise's penciled-in eyebrows shot up. "Well, that's wonderful, Susanna." She moved her gaze from the excited child to her mother. "Who's Melody?"

Josie's cheeks burned as she tried to explain. "Melody Lund. She used to babysit for one of Jacob's friends, which is how we know her. We saw her at the mall on Friday, and she invited us home to her parents' house for a few days." She laid her hand on Susanna's leg as if to correct her misconception of the situation. "We aren't living there, honey, just staying for a little while."

Louise's eyebrows returned to normal, and she smiled again, appearing much younger than her fifty-plus years. Josie had been surprised when she first found out her librarian friend was a day over thirty-five, as she certainly didn't look it, but Josie had decided the woman must have lived a relatively easy life. *That and she comes from good stock. But then, so do I. Mom held her age well, too, until she got sick. I might have done the same if I'd been able to continue living in a house instead of scrounging on the streets, trying to keep my children alive.*

Shaking off the self-pity that seemed to dog her every waking moment, she held her smile as she waited for Louise's response.

"I'm so glad to hear that," the librarian said. "I know the Lunds. Not well, but I've met them a couple of times over the years. Nice people."

She passed her smile from Jacob to Josie and, finally, to Susanna. "Well," she said, "I'd better get back to work. It's good to see you here again."

Josie nodded and watched her walk back toward the front desk. What she wouldn't give to have a pleasant, steady, respectable job like Louise's! She imagined it didn't pay a fortune, but it would certainly be sufficient to keep a roof over their heads and food on the table. But Josie had never worked or gotten a degree or even learned a trade. She'd married Sam during her second year at college, while she was still trying to figure out what she wanted to do with her life. Deep down, being a wife and mother was really the one desire she'd had for as long as she could remember, and when handsome, charismatic, fun-loving Sam Meyers began pursuing her, she said yes to his proposal and nearly ran down the aisle to marry him. True to his word, he had worked hard and provided her and their two children with a nice home and everything else she ever needed or wanted, allowing her to be a stay-at-home wife and mother. Life had been so good then . . . .

Then, she reminded herself. *Then, before the economy collapsed and Sam lost his job and didn't tell me. Then, before he cleaned out our savings and his retirement and even took out a second mortgage on the house so I'd think everything was fine while he pounded the pavement, looking for another job.*

Tears threatened, as she found herself wanting to scream at her dead husband. *Why, Sam? Even if you didn't want to tell me in the beginning, when you knew how sick you were—that you were dying—why didn't you tell me then? Why didn't you prepare me? I didn't even know how much money we owed. I had no idea we were beyond broke. How could you have let this happen to us?*

"Mom?"

Jacob laid his hand on her arm, and she realized she was trembling.

"Are you OK?"

She blinked back the tears and took a deep breath before gazing into her son's dark eyes. "I'm fine," she whispered. "Just . . . a little tired, I suppose." She smiled, her lips tight, as she did her best to calm herself.

Finally Jacob nodded and turned back to his book. She doubted he believed her, but he was sensitive enough to allow her to hold on to what little dignity she had left. There were times her seven-year-old son exhibited more maturity than his late father, whom he so resembled.

CHAPTER 7

Josie made a point of being back at the Lunds' in time to help Arlene with dinner. The rain was just turning from a fine mist to a steady downpour when they rang the front doorbell.

"Hey, you're back," Melody exclaimed, ushering them inside. "Mom's in the kitchen, and Dad's out in the garage, as usual." She laughed. "I think he'd live out there if Mom let him."

Josie and the kids stepped into the welcome warmth of the living room, and it crossed Josie's mind that she should have Jacob and Susanna settle down somewhere quietly. The house was small, and now that Todd was home and back in his bedroom, that left only the kitchen or living room, which doubled as their bedroom.

"Why don't you two sit down here on the couch," Josie suggested, helping them remove their jackets. She looked toward Melody for direction. "Um, where should I hang these? They're damp but not dripping."

"The back porch is fine," she said. "There are a couple of extra hooks by the door." She smiled down at Jacob and Susanna. "Did you guys have a good day?"

They nodded in unison. "We went to the library," Susanna announced.

"And other places," Jacob added, throwing his little sister a slightly condescending glance.

"Well," Melody said, "I've got to grab my stuff and head to class. See you all in a couple of hours." She spun on her heel and headed down the hallway to her room as Jacob and Susanna settled onto the couch.

"You can read while I help Mrs. Lund with dinner," Josie said, handing them each a book.

"I'm tired of reading," Susanna said. "We've been reading all day."

"Not all day," Jacob corrected. "Just for a few hours."

Susanna sighed. "That's almost all day, and I'm tired of it."

"Of course you are, my dear," Arlene said, coming in from the kitchen. "And I don't blame you one bit. Why don't I turn on the TV and you can watch cartoons while your mother and I peel potatoes." She cast a wary glance at Josie. "That is, if your mother doesn't mind . . . ?"

"Not at all," Josie said. "Thank you."

In moments the children were giggling along with Bugs Bunny and Daffy Duck, and Josie marveled that the old cartoons of her youth were still on television.

"Come and tell me about your day," Arlene said, leading Josie toward the sink where a small mound of spuds awaited them. "There's an extra paring knife in that drawer there, and you can put the peels in this bowl."

The familiarity of preparing dinner for her family sent the nearly ever-present lump back into Josie's throat, but she swallowed it and determined to tell her gracious hostess about all she'd discovered about homeschooling, thanks to Arlene's friend. As the two chatted, Josie almost convinced herself that their homeless days were over and life had taken a turn for the better. But the memory of standing in front of their repossessed home just a few months earlier, locked out and consigned to living wherever and however they could, was still too fresh to allow her hopeful thoughts to take root.

❄ ❄ ❄

Tuesday found the little family seated at a table toward the back of the library, a warm breakfast in their stomachs and sack lunches in their backpacks. Books and study materials were spread out on the table in front of them, and Josie rejoiced that all three of them were showered and dressed in clean clothes, with a promise of more clothes to come when they stopped by Arlene's church the next day. Their situation was better than it had been in quite awhile, but still Josie reined in her optimism. She knew how quickly things could deteriorate.

"Hey, there."

The male voice jolted Josie from her thoughts, as she realized she'd been staring at the same page for several minutes without absorbing anything she read. She raised her head just as Susanna squealed, "Rick! You're here!"

The grizzled old vet chuckled softly. "I sure am," he said, his voice only slightly above a whisper. "And I'm pleased to see you're here too." He leaned down a bit. "But we'd better remember this is a library and hold it down so they won't throw us out, eh?"

Susanna giggled and nodded.

"Rick," Jacob said, keeping his voice low, even as his face glowed in obvious pleasure. "We forgot to say good-bye to you when we left on Friday."

Josie's face warmed at her son's observation of their thoughtless oversight. *My thoughtless oversight,* she corrected herself. *I'm the grown-up here, and I'm the one who should have remembered to thank him for seeing that we had shelter that night.*

"No problem," Rick said. "I figured I'd run into you again one of these days." He smiled. "Glad to see you're all looking so well. Where are you staying now?"

"We live with the Lunds," Susanna announced.

Josie patted her daughter's leg. "We don't live with them," she reminded her, as her eyes darted from Rick to Susanna and back again. "We're just staying with them for a little while."

Rick's smile widened, temporarily erasing years from his face. "Hey, that's great! I figured when I hadn't seen you all weekend that something must have turned up."

"Where have you been staying?" Jacob asked.

The smile on Rick's face faded, and he shrugged. "Oh, around," he said, then turned his attention to the books spread across the table. "What's this? Homework?"

Jacob nodded. "Mom's homeschooling me."

"Me too," Susanna added.

Rick chuckled. "Well, now, that sounds like a great plan." He moved his gaze to Josie's face. "You're a good mom," he said, then shoved his hands into the pockets of his dirty jeans. "Well, I gotta run," he said. "They don't really like people like me hanging around at the library for too long. But I'm glad I decided to stop in and warm up for a few minutes. Good to see you all again."

"Wait a minute," Jacob said, scooting his chair back and standing up. "Why don't you stay and have lunch with us? We have plenty."

Rick raised his eyebrows. "Lunch? Oh no, I couldn't do that. You all eat your lunch, and I'll head downtown a ways. I can always find something down there."

Josie knew what he meant, even if her kids might not. Downtown there were always plenty of trash cans full of scraps that might fill a hungry mouth now and then, and the homeless didn't get hassled quite as much in that area.

"No," Josie said, surprised at the sound of her own voice. "Jacob is right. We have plenty. Please, stay and share our lunch with us. It's the least we can do after you got us into that warehouse the other night."

"Stay, Rick," Susanna added, her voice pleading. "Please?"

Josie watched the war of emotions play out on the man's face, and her heart went out to him. How well she understood his struggle between feeding a growling stomach and maintaining even a tiny shred of dignity. But she could tell her children had worn him down, as she turned to Jacob and said, "Bring another chair over, and we'll sit here together and have our sandwiches. Louise is working today, so she won't mind."

In moments the four of them were settled in, happily munching their food and talking in hushed tones. Josie had forgotten how good it felt to be the one offering help to someone else, rather than being the one receiving it. She smiled to realize Jacob and Susanna were experiencing that same joy, despite the fact that their lunch guest interrupted his meal often to cough into his handkerchief. So far Josie and the kids had stayed healthy, but she couldn't imagine how awful it must be to be homeless and sick at the same time.

※ ※ ※

By the time Friday rolled around, Josie could scarcely believe they had been living in the same place, with an actual roof over their head and three meals daily to keep their tummies full, for an entire week. The morning had dawned with a rare splash of sunlight, awakening Josie with what seemed to be a teasing promise of good things to come.

Fat chance, she thought, dragging herself from the couch. *I might have bought that last year, but not now; I know better.*

By the time she showered and dressed, the kids were awake and ready for breakfast. She told them to get ready while she went out to see if she could help Arlene in the kitchen.

"Good morning," she announced as she entered the cheerful little room, where Arlene stood at the counter pouring a cup of coffee. When she turned at the sound of Josie's voice, her face looked haggard. Had she not slept well? Josie frowned but kept the question to herself.

"Help yourself to coffee," Arlene said, her smile tight. "Oatmeal will be ready soon."

Josie nodded and went to the cupboard to snag a mug. She filled it with the steaming dark liquid and held it up to her face, inhaling deeply. How she loved the smell of coffee; sometimes she thought she liked the smell even more than the taste.

Turning back to the table, she saw that Arlene had already plunked herself down, so she sat down across from her. She knew the routine by now, meaning that Jerry had already gone to work and Melody and Todd had left for school. Josie tried to time her mornings so she and the kids wouldn't interfere with the Lunds as they got ready to start their day. Now they were all gone except Arlene, who stayed home during the day, earning a few extra dollars doing baking and ironing and other odd jobs for people. It wasn't much, she had explained to Josie, but it gave the family a little extra spending money without having to incur the expense of an additional vehicle and extra clothes to go out to work each day. Josie wished she'd at least have cultivated something like that during the years she was a stay-at-home mom and Sam was their sole source of income. *At least then I might have been able to postpone the inevitable and keep us in our house a little while longer.*

She took another sip of coffee and lifted her glance toward Arlene. The woman's gaze was already fixed upon her, and when their eyes met, Arlene quickly lowered hers. Something was wrong; Josie was sure of it now. And the sinking feeling in her stomach told her that whatever it was, one way or another it would lead to her and her children being out on the street once again.

CHAPTER 8

Despite Josie's misgivings, Saturday passed without incident, and by Sunday morning she had relaxed a bit, deciding Arlene's mood on Friday was just that—a mood. By that evening she'd seemed like her cheerful self again, and so Josie had dismissed her concerns. Still, she knew they couldn't stay with the Lunds forever, and she needed to do everything possible to have an alternative when the time came for them to move out. The problem was that she had no idea what those alternatives might be unless she was able to obtain some sort of housing through social services by then. Even saving money from her meager check wasn't much of an option, as she knew she'd have to pay something to the Lunds, at least enough to help cover the cost of food.

Once again sitting in the back of the Lunds' car with Susanna between her and Jacob, she wrestled with a sense of guilt over the imposition she and her children must be to their gracious guests. After all, both Melody and Todd had caught rides to church with friends. Though they all insisted it was what they often did anyway, Josie couldn't help but believe it was because they were making room for their guests.

We should have stayed home, Josie thought. *Then the Lunds could all have ridden together as a family—and I wouldn't have to go through the hypocrisy of sitting in church, pretending to worship and pray and believe that God really cares about us. But the kids wanted to go so badly. . . .*

Her thoughts drifted to her children's excited outbursts when they awoke and realized it was Sunday. She didn't have to do any prodding or cajoling to get them up and dressed that morning. But their exuberance would not influence her decision to pass on attending the evening service. She'd begged off the week before and would do the same tonight. Once a week was more than enough, at least so far as she was concerned.

Mr. Lund slowed as the church came into view. As he neared the driveway, his blinker clicking almost in time with the wipers that cleared the misty windshield as they pulled into the parking lot, Josie spotted the lady from the homeless shelter. She sighed. That was the problem with attending church regularly. You were forced to intermingle and converse with people, whether you wanted to or not. No doubt the woman would spot them and accost them with questions about where they were staying and how they were doing—and her talkative children would cheerfully oblige her with answers.

Invisible, she thought. *That's what I'd really like to be. At least as long as we're homeless. Who wants to be known as the homeless family?* Unbidden tears teased her eyes, but she blinked them away. *The homeless family. Well, why wouldn't we be known by that name? It's what we are, thanks to a husband who died without preparing me for what lay ahead, and a God who doesn't care enough to answer when I pray. So a homeless family is what we are. I know I should be thankful for a temporary place to stay for the time being, but it's just a matter of time until we're back out on the street again. Then what?*

No answer came, though she hadn't expected one. As the car came to a stop and Mr. Lund shut off the engine, she sighed and picked up her purse and Bible before opening the door and climbing out. She scarcely noticed the light rainfall that greeted her as she held the door for Susanna and watched Jacob get out on the other side. Taking a deep breath, she grabbed her daughter's hand and turned in the direction of the entrance, keeping a close eye on her son, who nearly skipped as he fell into place between Jerry and Arlene Lund. How easily and completely her children seemed to adapt to change! So much so that it concerned her. Despite the many times she'd cautioned them against thinking of the Lunds' home as their own, she knew that's exactly how they felt—and it had taken only slightly more than a week for that to happen.

❄ ❄ ❄

Though she blocked out most of the service, standing or sitting when instructed to do so and even mouthing a few words as they sang, Josie couldn't remember one point of the sermon—nor did she care to. She was just relieved when they were dismissed and she could escape into the aisle and toward the back door. Nudging her kids ahead of her, she was hopeful they would avoid the woman from the soup kitchen.

69

They were nearly at the exit when she spotted a familiar figure in a shabby green jacket scooting out ahead of them. He seemed to have been in a hurry and she hadn't seen his face, but she was relatively certain it was Rick.

So he comes to this church too. Wow. I knew this was a small town, but this is a bit much, even for Riverview. Now I have two people to avoid every week—well, so long as we're still with the Lunds, that is. And who knows how much longer that will be?

The rain had let up by the time they stepped outside, but the clouds still hung dark and heavy so she imagined the precipitation would start again at any moment. And why not? They lived in Washington after all. Rain was just a way of life there.

"I'm hungry," Susanna announced as they all piled into the car.

Josie felt the familiar flush creep into her cheeks. "Hush," Josie whispered. "Don't be rude, Susanna. We'll have lunch soon."

Arlene chuckled as she buckled herself into her seat. Turning back to look at Susanna, she smiled and said, "How about tomato soup and grilled cheese sandwiches?" she asked. "That was always one of my favorites on a cold day."

Susanna clapped her hands together. "Yes!" she shouted. "I love grilled cheese!"

"Then grilled cheese it is," Arlene said. "In fact, I believe I'll let you help me make them . . . if that's OK with your mom, of course."

Susanna gasped and turned her face upward toward Josie. Her blue eyes danced with excitement. "Can I, Mom? Can I help Mrs. Lund fix the sandwiches? Please? I'm big enough now. I'm five."

Josie tried to swallow the smile that teased her lips, but she couldn't do it. Giving in to the grin, she shook her head. "Yes, Susanna, I suppose you're right. You are big enough to help make lunch, aren't you? And so long as Mrs. Lund doesn't mind . . . ?" She ended her statement with a questioning glance toward the front seat.

Arlene turned back toward them, beaming. "Of course I don't mind. Melody's going to lunch with her friends, and Todd won't be home for a while either, so I can use all the help I can get."

Susanna chattered excitedly about "helping" and "cooking" all the way home, until Jacob rolled his dark eyes and leaned his head back against the seat. Josie knew he loved his sister dearly, but she imagined there were times it was trying to be a big brother.

❄ ❄ ❄

Lunch was over, and Susanna had done a surprisingly decent job of helping with the soup and sandwiches. Josie scolded herself for not having taught Susanna even the slightest bit about cooking while they still had a home of their own.

She wasn't even five then, she reminded herself. *It just never occurred to me that she was old enough to learn a few simple tasks. But she sure took to it with Arlene.*

The thought that Arlene was a better mother than she darted through Josie's mind and pierced her heart. How could she be a good mother when it took all her energy just to keep her children safe and fed?

Melody and Todd were still gone, so Arlene had suggested that Josie and the kids use Todd's room to take a nap. As Josie snuggled under a warm quilt on Todd's bed, with Susanna curled up beside her and Jacob already snoozing on the floor beside the closet, wrapped up in another quilt, Josie wished she could dismiss her concerns and drift off to sleep as quickly as her children. But how did she turn off the worries that plagued her? It was tough enough to fall asleep at night, and even more difficult in the subdued lighting of a gray Sunday afternoon.

At last she gave up and sneaked out of the room, silently shutting the door behind her. Maybe a hot cup of tea would help her relax.

Expecting the kitchen to be empty, Josie was surprised to hear Jerry and Arlene's hushed voices as she padded down the hallway. When Arlene mentioned Josie by name, she stopped, her heart thumping as she stood unmoving less than a foot from the kitchen doorway.

"But what are we going to do?" Arlene asked. "We can't just put them back out on the street. If we can keep them here at least through the holidays, maybe some housing will open up for them somewhere. Or maybe we can find someone at church

71

with a bigger house to take them in, someone who doesn't have a landlord to deal with."

Jerry's sigh was loud and long, and it was obvious he didn't enjoy the words he spoke. "I'd hoped we could do that, too, sweetheart. You know it's what I wanted from the moment they came here. And I thought surely we could keep them for a few more weeks before the landlord said anything. But somehow word got back to him, and the next thing I knew he called and asked if we had people living here with us. I told you then it could be a problem."

"I know. And I understand it's not your fault—or anyone's, for that matter. But when you told me on Friday morning, I was worried at first, even though I tried not to show it when Josie joined me for coffee. Then I spent most of the day praying about the situation, and I was so certain God would intervene and things would work out."

72

"I prayed that way too," Jerry said. "But now the landlord's called back and reminded me in no uncertain terms that our lease doesn't allow for anyone except our immediate family to live here."

Arlene's voice took on an imploring tone then as she asked, "But won't he listen to reason? Won't he at least consider letting them stay for a little while? Jerry, there are children involved here."

Jerry sighed again. "I know. And believe me, I'm going to do everything I can to try to find someone else to take them in, at least for a while. I'll call Pastor Jim first thing tomorrow morning if I don't get a chance to talk to him at church tonight."

"How . . . how long do you think we can get away with keeping them here?"

Josie imagined Jerry shrugging his shoulders as he answered. "A few days . . . maybe. But that's it. He was very clear about it, Arlene."

Josie felt light-headed as she turned and edged her way back to Todd's room. Opening the door, she gazed down at her sleeping children. How would she tell them that they had to leave this warm, safe place and go back out onto the streets to live? Sure, Jerry had said he'd ask the pastor about someone else taking them in, but she'd been that route with the pastor at the church she'd occasionally attended before. No way was she going to force some strangers to open their home to her and her kids. As awful as it would be, she'd rather sleep behind the cleaners than impose on people who didn't want them.

Besides, she had her December check and food vouchers now. Though she'd planned on offering some of it to the Lunds, she was glad she still had the entire amount. Maybe she could make it last a bit longer than usual. She'd heard there were always a few more beds open in shelters during the Christmas season, so if all went well, they might not have to spend many nights outside. And there was always the library during the day . . . .

Hot tears stung her eyes as she slipped into the room and closed the door behind her. A few more days. That didn't give them much time, so she'd better do whatever she could to prepare her children for the inevitable.

73

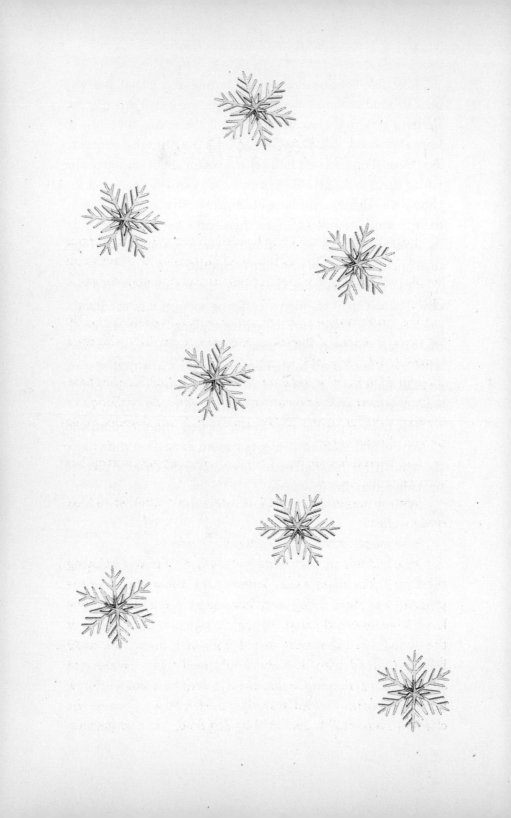

CHAPTER 9

The entire Lund family had headed off to the evening service at church, and just as Josie had suspected, without extra people to transport, the four of them had all ridden in the same car.

We've been nothing but a nuisance to them, Josie told herself, sitting on one end of the couch next to her children who were watching TV. *They look so comfortable and . . . oblivious,* she thought. *How in the world am I going to tell them? But they have to know sooner or later. I can't just wait until we're walking out the door with our jackets and backpacks and then announce that we won't be coming back.*

She cleared her throat. "So," she began, trying to keep her voice cheerful, "how do you like the program?"

Jacob shrugged. "It's good," he said as he continued to look straight ahead.

Susanna said nothing. Had she even heard?

Josie laid a hand on her daughter's arm. "Are you enjoying the show?" she asked again, knowing the answer because the program was about a dog, and Susanna adored animals of any kind. How Josie had hated leaving their golden lab, Mickey, at the pound when they were forced from their home, but she'd been concerned with how she would feed him. Having him along for protection was an incentive to keep him, but she knew her food vouchers would scarcely stretch to feed her and the children; she certainly couldn't buy dog food, too, and besides, they wouldn't have been able to bring him into the shelters. Still, though she knew she'd done what she must, every reminder of the once comfortable and normal life they'd known before tore at her heart, heaping additional weight to the already existing pile of guilt and regret.

Susanna glanced up at her before returning her gaze to the TV screen. "I love it," she said. "It's about a dog."

Josie nodded. Just as she'd suspected. It would be so much easier to let them watch their program and then make up the sofa bed and put them down for the night without saying anything. But would it be any easier tomorrow? She doubted it.

"Kids," she said, "I've been thinking that . . . maybe we should consider . . . leaving here soon. I mean, we can't stay with the Lunds forever. They've been very kind to us, but . . . it's not fair to them for us to take advantage."

She had the attention of both children now, as they stared up at her, wide-eyed.

Jacob frowned. "What are you talking about, Mom? Why would we leave here? Where would we go?"

Susanna's face puckered as tears pooled in her eyes. "I don't want to leave," she whimpered. "I like it here. And Mrs. Lund says I'm a good helper in the kitchen." She shook her head. "We're not taking 'vantage. They want us here!"

Josie's heart squeezed. Oh, how she'd rather rip out her tongue than have this conversation with her children!

"I'm not saying they don't want us," she said, once again laying her hand on Susanna's arm. "I'm just saying—"

"No!" Susanna shook off her mother's hand and jumped to her feet. "I won't go! I'm not going to sleep behind that creepy laundry anymore, and I don't want to be hungry and dirty ever again. No, I won't go! I won't!"

The red-faced child raced from the room, down the hall, and into the bathroom, where she slammed the door behind her.

Josie heard the lock click, and she knew the discussion, at least so far as Susanna was concerned, was over.

*   *   *

By the time Susanna finally came out of the bathroom, Josie had made up the sofa bed and turned off the TV. Susanna climbed in wordlessly and pulled the covers over her head. Within moments her steady breathing told Josie her daughter was asleep.

Though it was difficult to deal with Susanna's emotional outbursts, Josie understood them. How many times had she felt like doing the same? But she couldn't, of course. Someone had to exhibit control and confidence, and that someone was her—whether she had any or not.

Jacob had not spoken a word since Susanna ran off to the bathroom. When Josie told him it was time for bed, he had lain down without protest. Neither child had asked her to read a story, which was a custom Josie had tried to maintain whenever possible, even on the street. If they were somewhere too dark to read, she told a story from memory or made one up. The only time she changed her routine was when they were in a shelter that required lights out early and then no talking. Still, as much as it hurt that her children had not requested a story this night, she was also relieved, as she wondered if she could have gotten through one without breaking down completely.

I'm so tired of having to be strong, she thought, flipping off the light and crawling into bed between the children. *I'm tired of smiling and pretending and encouraging and promising. I'm tired of everything! But what else can I do? They need me. They're so tiny and . . . helpless.*

The tears came then, and once again she flipped onto her stomach and sobbed into the pillow, hoping Susanna and Jacob wouldn't hear her. When she heard the Lunds' car pull in and the family come in from the garage to the kitchen, she nearly stuffed the pillow in her mouth to stifle her sobs. With every ounce of self-discipline she contained, she lay still and quiet until the family had peeled off and gone to their rooms. How would she ever carry this off tomorrow? Determined not to let on to the Lunds that she knew their dilemma, she promised herself she would find a way.

❄ ❄ ❄

Monday morning breakfast had come and gone without incident, but the tension had kept Josie's stomach in a knot. She'd forced down a cup of coffee and a couple of bites of toast, but had to pass on the eggs and bacon.

Arlene had smiled and chatted as if everything were normal, but Josie imagined that was for the children's sake. She truly was a dear and kind woman, but Josie understood there was nothing the poor lady could do about the situation. Maybe she was holding off telling her in hope that God would come through with a miracle, though Josie wasn't holding her breath on that one.

Her biggest concern was that one of the kids might say something about their conversation the night before, and then Arlene would suspect that Josie had been eavesdropping on her and Jerry. Thankfully, Jacob and Susanna had said nothing about it, though they weren't as chipper as usual.

The previous week, when Josie thought they would be staying at the Lunds a while longer, she had splurged with a couple dollars of her December check and loaded the three of them onto the bus for the ride to and from the library when it was raining. Today, though the mist was cold and steady, she insisted they use the umbrellas they had picked up at Arlene and Jerry's church when they'd dropped by there a few days earlier and raided the clothes closet. Now Josie wondered how they were going to carry their extra clothing around when they were on the streets again.

As they trudged along in near silence, Josie knew her children hadn't forgotten their discussion the night before. Just because neither of them had mentioned it didn't mean the topic wasn't swirling around in their thoughts. Had she done more harm than good by mentioning it before it was necessary?

Turning right at the corner, she spotted the library in the distance. It would be good to get inside where it was warm and dry, but she wondered how much studying they'd get done. Certainly their hearts wouldn't be in it, as each contemplated what lay ahead. Did her little ones realize their days at the Lunds' house were numbered, or were they clinging to the hope that she'd simply been presenting a possibility and would now dismiss it?

If only it were that easy, she thought. *How do I explain to them that it's not up to me? It's not my choice—and it's not my fault!*

Blinking away tears, she watched Jacob pull open the library door and wait as she and Susanna entered. Her children deserved so much better than what she gave them, but what was she to do? There truly seemed to be no answer.

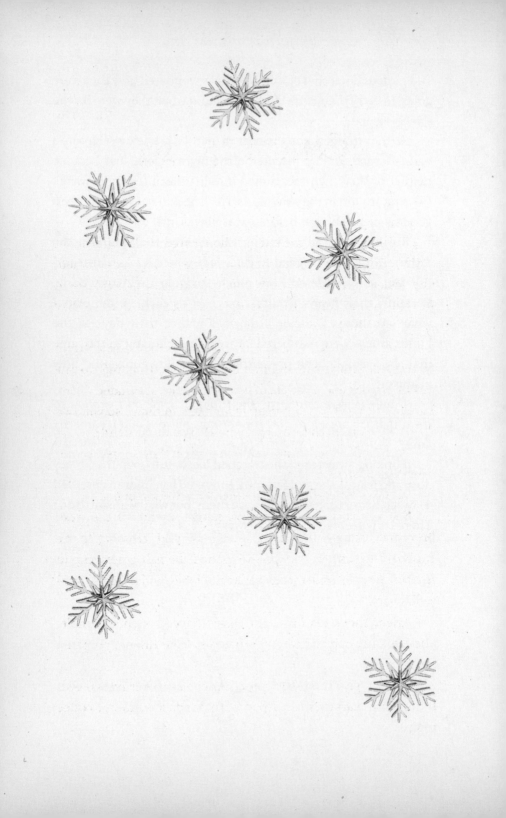

CHAPTER 10

W hen Josie and the kids got home Wednesday afternoon, Arlene was waiting for them. Her eyes were red-rimmed, and Josie realized she'd been crying. When she asked Josie to put the kids in Todd's room to play and close the door so they could talk, she knew it wasn't good.

"You can watch TV later," Josie said as she escorted Jacob and Susanna down the hall and into the bedroom. Handing them a box of crayons and a couple of coloring books, she added, "Mrs. Lund and I need to talk privately for a few minutes, so you two stay in here until I come and get you. Do you understand?"

Both nodded solemnly, and Josie knew they sensed something was wrong.

"Coffee?" Arlene asked as Josie entered the kitchen.

She was about to decline but caught a whiff of the fresh brew and changed her mind. "Sure," she said, crossing to the cupboard to retrieve a mug. She spotted the half empty cup in front of Arlene, who already sat at the table, and asked, "Can I refill yours?"

Arlene shook her head, and Josie noticed her chin tremble. She filled her cup and sank down across from Arlene, prepared for the worst.

"I . . . I have some bad news," Arlene said, her brown eyes filling with tears as she clasped both hands around her coffee mug.

Josie dropped her gaze to her own cup. She'd known this was coming, but she'd hoped something might happen to change it—prolong it, at least. But now, here it was. She took a deep breath and looked up. "We have to leave, don't we?"

The tears spilled over onto Arlene's cheeks then, and she nodded. "Yes," she said, her voice cracking. "And so much sooner than I'd hoped. I . . . " She swallowed. "I knew you couldn't stay indefinitely, but I thought at least through the holidays. But now . . . "

Her voice trailed off as she fought visibly for control. Josie sensed she should go to her and offer comfort, but she felt paralyzed to do so. How much more bad news could she be expected to accept?

"Our landlord knows you're here and is not being flexible about it at all. He has clearly reminded us of the terms of our lease, and . . . " Another sigh before she continued. "But Jerry and I have been talking, and we just can't put you and the children out on the street. We're going to try to put the landlord off as long as possible, and then . . . then maybe we can come up with something else. We've talked to the pastor, and he's going to check with some people at church, and . . . if that doesn't work, then Jerry and I are thinking we could use some of our savings to help you get a place, at least for a while, and—"

Josie felt her eyes widen. The Lunds would dip into what she was sure were meager savings for her and her children? It was an incredible gesture, but one she could never allow them to make.

"No," she said, shaking her head and putting out her hand as if to stop the conversation from going any further. "No, Arlene. I could never let you do that. You've already been so very kind to us, and we appreciate it more than you know, but we could never use your savings. I can only imagine how hard the two of you have worked to build it up, and besides, you have two children of your own to think of." She paused and shook her head again. "No, it's not an option. But thank you so very much for offering."

Arlene snagged a tissue from the box on the far side of the table and dabbed at her face. "I knew you'd say that," she said, "but the offer is open. Please think about it. You can't possibly take those babies back out on the street. Surely we can keep you here long enough to find something else!"

Josie hoped Arlene was right, but past experience didn't line up with that hope. Terror like a dark cloud seemed to rise up and hover over her, making it hard to speak or think. Everything in her wanted to cry out, "Yes, we'll take your money. We'll take anything we can to keep from living on the streets again." But she pressed her lips together, refusing to give in to such selfish sentiments. She might have lost her mother, her husband, her home, and even her dignity, but she would not lose her decency. The weeping woman who sat across from her deserved to be treated as kindly as she treated others.

Forcing herself to move, Josie finally got up from her seat and went to kneel beside Arlene Lund. Wordlessly they fell into one another's arms and cried.

❄ ❄ ❄

Josie managed to collect herself and splash enough cold water on her eyes that when she returned to Todd's room the children weren't alarmed at her appearance. But she knew they weren't fooled by her forced cheerfulness either.

How much should she tell them? She still wasn't sure, but she was past the point of hoping she could avoid it indefinitely. At best they could hold out for a couple more days before they dipped into their meager funds to rent a cheap motel room or found themselves sleeping in a shelter or behind the cleaners again.

"What did Mrs. Lund want to talk about?" Susanna asked, her face pale as she peered up at her mother.

Josie swallowed the returning lump in her throat and took a deep breath. "Come sit down by me," she said, settling onto the edge of the bed. Heads drooping, the children sat down, one on each side of her.

She put her arms around them, reminding herself that she owed it to them to be honest. Still, she had to fight the idea of downplaying the entire incident by telling them Arlene had just been trying to convince her and the children to join them for Wednesday night service — an invitation that actually had come up and she promptly declined. Dismissing such a cowardly and deceptive approach, she said, "You know I've told you since we came here that staying with the Lunds was temporary, right?"

They nodded, and Josie steeled herself to continue. "It seems the Lunds' landlord has a condition in their rental lease that says no one outside their immediate family of four can live here."

"But we're not living here," Susanna whined. "We're just staying. You said so, Mommy."

Josie tried to smile. "Technically you're right, honey. We're not living here. But apparently the landlord feels visitors shouldn't be here for more than a few days at the most. And now he's putting pressure on Mr. and Mrs. Lund to move us out."

Susanna's blue eyes filled and her lower lip trembled. "That's mean," she said.

Josie pulled her close. "I'm sure he doesn't intend for it to be," she said, hoping she sounded convincing. "It's just something landlords have to do sometimes. And we don't want to cause the Lunds any trouble now, do we?"

Susanna dropped her gaze to her lap and shook her head, but her shoulders shook and Josie knew her daughter was on the edge of a full-blown sob-fest. Jacob, on the other hand, sat silently, though she felt him stiffen in her grasp.

"When do we have to leave?" he asked at last, not looking at her when he spoke.

"Soon," she said, her own voice shaking by then. "In a few days at the most."

Susanna looked back up, and Josie's heart ached at the tears streaming down the girl's cheeks. "Does that mean we won't be able to go to church with them anymore or go Christmas caroling?"

Josie fought to prevent the sob from escaping her chest, though it felt as if it would explode her rib cage in the process. "I don't know," she whispered. "I don't know, baby."

Susanna buried her face in her mother's lap and wailed, while Josie wondered just how much worse things could get before she simply gave up and died of a broken heart.

※ ※ ※

Karen never missed a Wednesday night service, and tonight was no exception. Though the weather was near freezing outside, she bundled up, grabbed her Bible, and headed off to church. Along the way she spotted Rick, hunched against the wind and rain but obviously heading in the same direction as she.

"Hey there," she called, pulling over to the side of the road and hitting the down button on the passenger-side window. "Headed for church?"

Rick glanced up, breaking into a smile when he spotted her. "Sure am," he said. "You too?"

"Me too. Come on, jump in. No sense getting any colder or wetter than you already are."

In seconds Rick had climbed in and shut the door behind him, rubbing his hands together in front of the warm air coming from the dashboard vents. "Oh man, does that feel good!"

Karen smiled. "It's nasty out there tonight, isn't it?"

Rick nodded and waited to speak until his coughing spell subsided. "Yes, ma'am, it sure is. I can't thank you enough for stopping to pick me up."

The realization that attending church meant so much to Rick that he would venture out into such awful weather, particularly with his health as it was, touched Karen's heart. Occasionally she was tempted to feel sorry for herself as she thought back over her many years alone and the lost dreams she'd once shared with a man she loved deeply, but then she saw someone like Rick, who had nowhere to lay his head at night and had to trust God for every meal, and she quickly asked the Lord to forgive her selfishness.

"You know," she said, "I go to church every Sunday morning and evening, plus Wednesday evening, and several other times each week, depending on what's going on over there. You're more than welcome to hitch a ride with me anytime. I could give you my cell number so we could connect in case I'm not at home, and then we can figure out where I could pick you up."

Rick paused a moment before answering. "I . . . don't usually have access to a phone," he said, coughing again. "But if you're sure you don't mind, I could just stop by your house and catch a ride if you're there. If not, no big deal. It's not like it's out of my way or anything, and I'm usually closer to your place than the church, so that would be great."

Karen felt her cheeks burn and was glad the darkness of night didn't allow Rick to see her embarrassment. How spoiled and naïve was she that she just assumed everyone had a cell phone? After working with the homeless as long as she had, surely she knew better!

She swallowed before answering. "That would be fine, Rick," she said. "Just drop by about a half hour or so before service, and I'm almost always there, getting ready to leave. I'd enjoy the company. And . . . " She hesitated before continuing. "And I'd be happy to give you a ride . . . home." The final word echoed in the dead air around her, and she wished she'd verbalized her offer differently.

"Thanks," Rick said. "I usually hang out in the same areas, so you can always just drop me off nearby. I appreciate it."

She knew he meant it, and his humble appreciation burned in her heart. She'd been volunteering at shelters for years, and yet she realized she still had so very much to learn about—and from—the people who stayed in them.

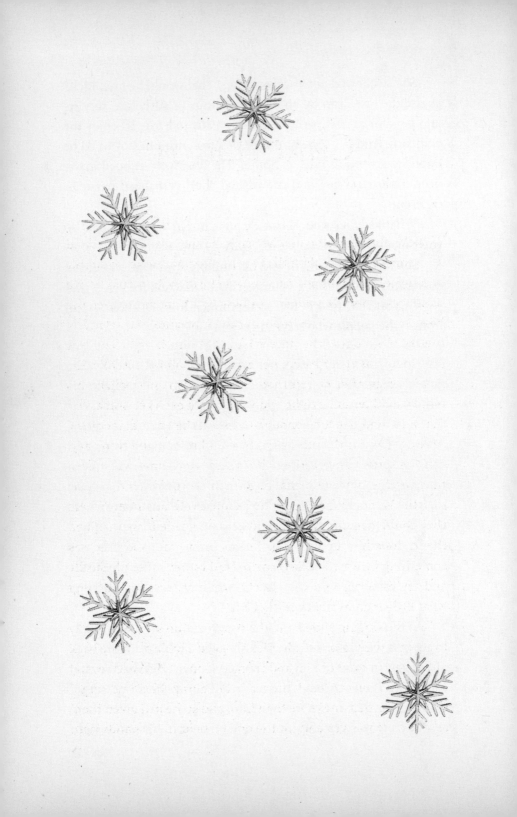

CHAPTER 11

Rick's chest hurt too much to sing, but he closed his eyes and worshiped silently with the congregation. He kept a supply of cough drops in his pocket whenever he knew he would be in a public place, but they weren't helping much anymore. Even the heavy-duty cough syrup he got at the VA hospital was relatively useless these days. The doctor had told him it would be this way, so he wasn't surprised, nor even disappointed actually. His greatest fear, after he returned from Vietnam and realized his mind would never be right again and might even get worse, was that he would live long enough to lose all his mental faculties. At least now, for the most part, he could reason and think and carry on brief conversations. But there were times when even that became more of a challenge than he could handle. If he took the VA doctor's advice to check into a veterans' home where they could give him the physical care he needed, he imagined they'd dope him up on drugs for his brain, too, and that was something he wasn't willing to do. He'd rather suffer physically and try to survive on the streets, while at least maintaining what little mental clarity he had left.

As the singing ended and the congregation sat down, ready to get into the pastor's study, Rick snagged a Bible from the back of the pew in front of him and cracked it open. He'd had several of his own Bibles through the years, but always he found someone who needed one more than him, and so he had given them all away. He was grateful for the one he held in his hands right now, as he had grown to appreciate the power of God's Word. Even when he didn't have a copy of the Scriptures with him and even when he had his worst periods of feeling confused and out of touch, the many verses he'd memorized over the years would rise up in his heart and give him comfort. One day very soon, he knew for certain, both his mind and body would be healed when he crossed that line into eternity and stood in the presence of his Savior.

As the pastor instructed the congregation where to turn, Rick cut his eyes to the side to glance at the lady named Karen, who had been so kind to him. Several times she'd given him a ride or offered him some food—even taking him home with her on occasion to share a meal with her. He knew that was something volunteers were discouraged from doing, and he certainly understood why, but it meant a lot to him that she would invite him into her car or her home. He'd heard somewhere that her husband had died many years earlier, and he marveled that such a gracious lady had never remarried.

I'm her Husband.

The words echoed in his heart, and Rick felt the sting of hot tears, even as the truth penetrated his thoughts. Why would she settle for an imperfect human husband when she could have the only perfect One to love and care for her? It was obvious Karen had made a wise choice.

Within moments Rick was lost in the Bible study, turning pages and jotting notes on the back of an offering envelope. Even if he didn't go back and read his notes later, he found that writing down the key words helped him retain the message.

By the time the service drew to a close, Rick was struggling to keep himself from erupting into a major coughing fit. "Excuse me," he whispered to Karen. "I've got to step outside before I start coughing. I'll wait for you there."

The cold, damp air slapped his face as he eased his way out the door and stood under the overhang. Looking out into the cold, dark night, he felt a momentary temptation to at least consider trying to get into one of those veterans' homes. If nothing else, he'd be warm and dry. But did he really want to go there and spend his last days on earth as a drugged-up zombie?

He shook his head. He definitely did not. Whatever the streets held for him, he would trust God to get him through what little was left of his life. His Lord had never let him down before, and he knew He would carry him the rest of the way.

People were streaming out the doors now, talking and laughing as they opened umbrellas and pulled coats tight before stepping out into the threatening weather. Karen was one of the last to exit, and she immediately apologized the moment she spotted him.

"I'm so sorry to keep you waiting," she said. "I ran into the Lunds—you know, the people the little Meyers family has been staying with—and Arlene told me her landlord is forcing them to put Josie and the kids out."

Under the outdoor lights of the church, Rick detected the hint of tears in Karen's gray eyes. Her slightly plump face looked ready to crumple, even as his own heart began to ache. It was bad enough that people like him had to survive in the treacherous elements of a Pacific Northwest winter, but a woman and two small children should never be subjected to such misery.

"That's not right," he said. "I was so glad when I heard they had somewhere to stay. Surely there's somebody here in the church who can help."

Karen nodded. "I'm thinking the same thing. Arlene says the pastor is checking, but if it doesn't work out I could probably take them in for a few days. Technically, I'm not supposed to, of course, but maybe . . . " Her voice trailed off.

"Yeah," Rick said. "Maybe." He saw that she was shivering then and said, "Come on. Let's get in the car before you catch cold. Maybe we can spend a few extra minutes praying for Josie and the kids before we leave."

She turned and started down the steps, with Rick at her side. "Good idea," she said. "Surely God will show us what to do . . . or provide something for them, or . . . "

Rick's cough erupted before she could complete her thought, and he sighed with relief as he slid into the passenger seat of Karen's car. He just wished there was something he could do personally, but in his position, what did he have to offer anyone?

❄ ❄ ❄

Friday night was dismal — not just because of the dreary weather but because Josie knew they were running out of time. Arlene had told her the landlord was coming by on Sunday to confirm they had "taken care of the lease agreement issue," which meant Josie and the kids had to be out by then.

I suppose I should be grateful for the last couple of weeks here, she thought as she lay on her back on the sofa bed between her sleeping children, staring at a ceiling she could just barely make out in the near darkness. *I know it's not Arlene and Jerry's fault. They've been wonderful, and so have their kids. But now what? Is it really better to find temporary shelter, only to have to return to the streets, than just to accept that we're homeless, period?*

She thought of the news Arlene had given her just moments before they all turned in for the night. Though the pastor hadn't come up with anything yet, at least so far as a place for them to stay, he had promised a small amount of cash from their emergency fund. In addition, the woman named Karen, whom they'd met at the soup kitchen and then seen again at church, had offered to let Josie and the kids stay with her for a few days while they looked for something else. But Josie knew what that meant, and she wasn't going to put her children through that sort of disappointment again. Getting attached to people and homes, even beds and regular meals, was devastating when it was ripped away.

No. False hope was worse than sleeping behind the cleaners. At least she had nearly her full December check left, since the Lunds hadn't allowed her to pay them anything for room or board while they were there, plus the cash the pastor had offered. That meant, if she budgeted carefully, they would be able to spend most nights between now and the New Year in cheap motels. Her food vouchers would keep them from starving, and Arlene had encouraged them to come by for dinner as often as they liked.

It wasn't much of a plan, but it was all she had. As she listened to the wind howl outside, she snuggled deeper under the covers, realizing they had only one more night with the Lunds before they'd have to move on. Where would they be sleeping on Sunday night? The thought drove any possibility of sleep far from her mind.

❋ ❋ ❋

Josie hadn't heard one word the pastor spoke, nor paid attention to any of the songs or announcements or prayers. If it had been strictly up to her, they would have skipped church entirely, but Jacob and Susanna had once again begged to go, and so she had relented. Before leaving that morning, however, she'd made sure all their belongings—the ones they could carry with them, anyway—were loaded into the trunk of the Lund family's car so Jerry and Arlene could drop them off near the mall after church. Arlene had packed them all a huge lunch and reminded them that their house was open to them for dinner anytime. And then they'd all climbed in the car and headed to church, where they'd scrunched into a pew together, with Melody and Todd joining them rather than sitting with their friends. Josie thought it was one of the more heartbreaking scenarios she'd witnessed in the last few nightmare months of her life.

As they moved down the aisle toward the exit, Josie felt a hand on her shoulder. Surprised, she turned to find Karen standing directly behind her. Once again, as had happened the first time she saw Karen at the soup kitchen, Josie thought of her aunt Jeneen, but quickly dismissed the comparison. She knew why Karen had stopped her, and she'd been dreading it.

"Can I talk with you a minute?" Karen whispered, leaning close.

Josie felt her cheeks flush. "Arlene told me," she said. "About your kind offer, I mean. About letting us stay with you for a few days." She swallowed. "I . . . just don't think it's a good idea. We did that with Arlene and Jerry, and though I warned them not to, the kids got comfortable there and started to think of it as their home. Now we have to leave and go back on the streets. I just can't put them through that again."

Karen's gray eyes misted over, and she nodded. "I understand," she said. "But . . . please, won't you reconsider? Even a few days are better than none. I just wish I could make it a permanent offer, but I'd lose my position as a volunteer. We're just not supposed to do that. You understand, don't you?"

Josie nodded. She truly did understand. How could a volunteer justify taking in one family and leaving the others out in the cold? But it was good of her to offer.

"Thanks," Josie said. "But really, I think it's better if we don't. We'd just be postponing the inevitable. Besides, I do have a little money—most of my December check and some cash from your pastor, and also some food vouchers. We'll be OK."

A flicker of doubt crossed Karen's face, and she sighed before pulling a card from her pocket. "All right. But here, let me give you my number and address. The offer stands, and if you end up with nowhere to go some night, you can come over. Or call me and I'll pick you up."

Josie's eyes stung with unwanted tears, and she mumbled a thank-you as she took Karen's card and shoved it in her coat pocket. She doubted she'd take her up on her offer, but who knew what might happen if she and the children got desperate enough?

Turning away before she lost control completely, she hurried to catch up with Susanna and Jacob and the Lunds. They had one final ride to take before Jerry and Arlene dropped them off in the thin Washington sunshine.

At least it's not raining, she told herself, and took a deep breath as she started down the steps toward the parking lot.

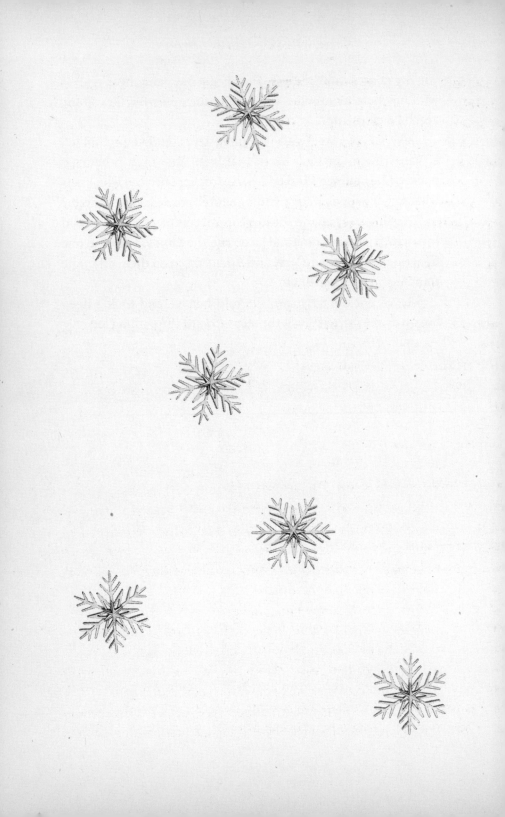

CHAPTER 12

They all tried desperately but failed miserably to maintain their composure when the Lunds stopped the car in an area known for cheap motel rooms. It was also known for drugs and prostitution, a fact Josie tried to block from her mind as Jerry helped her unload the trunk. Josie handed the children their backpacks and strapped on her own, thanking their benefactors again for allowing them to store things at their home.

A car pulled up behind them, and Josie turned to see Todd and Melody climbing out, leaving one of their friends at the wheel. Apparently they had followed the Lunds' car so they could say good-bye. The tears Josie had been struggling to hold back spilled from her eyes then, as she realized how much easier it would have been for the teenagers to avoid this scene.

But they came anyway, she thought, swiping at her tears with her jacket sleeve. *That's the kind of people the Lunds are. I didn't realize until now how much I would miss them!*

Jacob spotted Melody and ran into her arms, as she pulled him tight and closed her eyes—no doubt blinking back tears, too, Josie thought. Susanna clung to Mr. Lund's leg as she used to do with her own father, and once again Josie confirmed her belief that as nice as the temporary stay had been, her children's suffering was compounded by yet another separation.

Arms encircled Josie from behind, and she turned to find herself staring into Arlene's wet, gray eyes. How dear this woman had become to her over the past couple of weeks! Sitting together at her kitchen table as they sipped coffee and chatted had brought at least a sliver of healing to Josie's sorrow, but now it seemed her sorrow would be restored with a vengeance.

The two women hugged and cried, until Jerry joined them and called the rest to do the same. "We need to pray together," he said. "There is nothing any of us can do to change this situation, but God is sovereign. He loves each of us more than we can begin to imagine, and we need to trust Him to work this out for good."

Josie's heart screamed in rebellion at the mention of a loving God and His goodness, but she couldn't bring herself to offend the Lunds in any way. The little group joined hands as Jerry offered up a brief but heartfelt prayer to the God he so obviously believed was listening—and would respond.

"Dear heavenly Father," he said, "You promised that wherever two or more of us are gathered together in Your name, You are there with us. Well, here we are, Lord, and we welcome You here. We know You love us, Father—each one of us—more than we can ever begin to imagine. For that, Lord, we truly thank You, for we know we don't deserve Your love—or Your mercy or forgiveness or anything besides Your wrath. And yet You have provided all we need through the death and resurrection of Your only Son, our Lord Jesus Christ. Because of that great sacrifice, we come to You in Jesus' name, humbly asking for a miracle of care and provision for Josie, Susanna, and Jacob. We don't know what that looks like, Father, or how or when or where it will come. But we know You are faithful and Your Word is true, so we are trusting You to answer, Lord. And we thank You now for doing so. In Christ's name we pray, amen."

Despite her resistance to Jerry's continued references to God as good and loving, Josie couldn't deny the inexplicable sense of peace that flowed over her as she absorbed the words of his prayer. Was it possible God truly was listening? Did she dare even hope for an answer . . . or was she just setting herself and her children up for yet another disappointment?

As the little prayer circle broke up and exchanged final hugs before the Lunds piled back in their cars and drove away, Josie stood on the sidewalk, an arm around each child as they watched the vehicles turn the corner and disappear from sight. Once again they were alone, with nightfall only hours away. The dark clouds that had begun to gather in the distance were moving in, ready to block out the sun and, with it, the brief feeling of peace that had offered Josie a glimmer of hope.

※ ※ ※

Josie's eyes felt as if she'd rubbed them with emery boards when she awoke to the familiar sound of rain on Monday morning. Squinting in the gray light, she took in her unfamiliar surroundings, her heart sinking as she realized where they were.

Taking a quick headcount, she confirmed that the children were both sound asleep, squeezed onto the one double bed with her, all huddled under the covers in a cheap motel room with a heater that hummed and banged most of the night but put out little warmth.

The heater, however, had been the least of Josie's concerns as she tried in vain to fall asleep the night before. They had opted for the cheapest place they could find that still had some semblance of cleanliness and safety to it, but the noise from the parking lot and surrounding rooms had kept her awake until the early predawn hours.

She glanced at Susanna, her blonde hair splayed across the pillow and her face peaceful. Thank goodness her children seemed able to sleep nearly anywhere and through almost any type of noise. Susanna had awakened at one point, though, needing to use the bathroom. When she returned to bed she rubbed her eyes and asked her mother, "How come everybody's always yelling and playing music out there? Aren't motels for sleeping?"

Josie had bitten back the words that would have explained to her what other activities motels often facilitated. Instead she had assured her that everything was fine and rubbed her back until the girl was once again asleep.

All was quiet now, except for occasional bursts of noise from the heater, which seemed so ill-equipped to do its job. Still, it was warmer by quite a few degrees in here than outside, and there was at least some level of safety within the room. For that Josie was grateful.

She took mental stock of the food they had with them. The Lunds had packed up a big sack full of sandwiches that wouldn't spoil quickly, plus dried and fresh fruit. If they used it wisely, it should last for two or even three days. And they did still have all their food vouchers, plus some cash. It was possible they could afford to rent a room nearly every night this month, though January would be another story entirely.

Can't let myself think about that. For now we're somewhat safe and warm, and we have food. That's better than some nights since we've been homeless.

The thought crossed her mind, too, that there was always the slim chance they could get into a shelter for a few nights, which would enable her to make their existing funds stretch even further. Oh, if only winter didn't last so long in the Pacific Northwest! It would be months before she could even hope for a reprieve from this cold, damp weather, not to mention that the next couple of months brought the very real possibility of ice and snow.

I've got to make sure we have enough set aside to get into a room somewhere if that happens, she told herself, *even if it means spending most nights in shelters or even a night or two behind the cleaners when the weather's not so bad.*

Jacob sighed and rolled toward her, throwing his arm across her in the process. Josie turned her head and gazed at him—the man-child who wanted so much to be a grown-up and to help. "My baby," she whispered. "You're still just a baby, sweet Jacob."

She smiled then, realizing she only got away with saying that because he was asleep. How he would have been insulted if he had heard her!

These are the best times, she thought, *when my children are sleeping and not aware of where they are. Sometimes I wish we could all just go to sleep and never wake up.*

※　※　※

One of the things Josie hated most about cheap motels in the bad area of town was that she was hesitant to let the children leave the room, even for a few minutes. But housekeeping did not come with the rental, and if she wanted clean towels or sheets, she had to venture out long enough to pick them up at the office. Besides, she also had to decide daily if she was going to fork over more money for another night or save what little funds she had and move on somewhere else.

She wrestled with that very decision today, and yet the continuing rain and near-freezing temperatures discouraged her from leaving. And though she'd prefer to spend the day at the library rather than cooped up where they were, she wondered at the wisdom of wasting money on bus fare. Perhaps they really would be better off staying right where they were. After all, if they kept their jackets on or stayed under the blankets, the heater worked well enough to keep them fairly warm. And in between the children's studies, they could watch TV, though she limited the amount of time and type of programs involved.

After a cold breakfast of peanut butter and jelly sandwiches and oranges, Josie got the kids started reading and then instructed them to work quietly while she went to the front office to exchange their dirty towels for clean ones and to pay another night's rent.

Susanna's face fell at the announcement, and she immediately jumped up from the bed where she had been propped against the wall, looking through her picture book. "I want to go with you!" she cried. "I don't want to stay here by myself."

Josie stroked her hair. "I'll only be a few minutes," she soothed. "And you won't be alone. Jacob will stay here with you."

The child turned her face upward and shook her head vehemently. "No," she insisted. "I want to come with you. And I want Jacob to come too." Tears were already forming on her dark lashes. "I don't like it here. It's noisy and scary. There's bad people out there."

Josie's heart skipped a beat. In all the time they'd spent on the street or in shelters, Susanna had never said anything about "bad people." Was it possible her daughter sensed the evil and perversity that went on in some of the rooms around them?

Nodding, Josie conceded. "All right," she said. "You and Jacob put on your shoes and zip your jackets. We'll all go down to the office together. It might do you good to get some fresh air for a few minutes, even if it is cold and wet. But back to your books as soon as we're done."

The children readily agreed, and Josie was surprised that even Jacob seemed relieved to be coming with her. Suddenly she was glad the one thing that seemed to be in good working order in this run-down establishment was the set of three inside locks on the door.

CHAPTER 13

Tuesday morning dawned bright and sunny, though pierced by an icy wind. Still, Josie decided not to spend another day locked up in their room or even renewing it yet. By check-out time they were bundled up and ready to hike the ten or so blocks to the library. They'd be cold and tired by the time they got there, but they still had enough sandwiches and fruit for the day, and there was a water fountain in the building, so it would be worth the effort. Josie would make sure they left in plenty of time to stop by the one shelter she knew of that gave priority to families with small children—if they arrived in time. The problem was they didn't open the doors until four thirty, but after that it was first-come, first-served. Chances were slim they'd get in, but she figured it was worth trying before shelling out more money for another night in a tawdry motel.

"We look like Rudolph the Red-Nosed Reindeer," Susanna announced as they mounted the library steps after their brisk walk. Josie glanced at her children's red noses and cheeks and laughed. "You're right," she said, herding them inside.

Few people occupied the tables and chairs scattered throughout the cozy room, though the half-dozen computers were all in use. Josie had expected as much and settled herself and the kids into a table toward the back. She could see the computer stations from there, and if one opened up she just might try to get on it. It was silly, she knew, but each time she found herself with computer access she checked her email, though she wondered how long unused free accounts remained active before they were shut down. She hadn't received anything but junk in weeks, but curiosity and a lingering tie to her past life seemed to call her—not to mention the fact that she'd given her email address to social services for an alternate contact to her post office box.

I should get the kids involved on the computer, too, she reminded herself. *Especially Jacob. They'll need it for homework in the future.*

The memory of the state-of-the-art computer system Sam had set up for them in their bedroom flitted through her mind, but she dismissed it as quickly as it came. Like so much of her other furniture and belongings, she'd sold that computer for pennies on the dollar, just to try to make one more mortgage payment before the bank repossessed their home. In the end, she'd run out of things to sell, and she'd left her home behind, taking only those things that mattered most—Susanna and Jacob, and the few very basic necessities they could carry in their backpacks.

Nothing much has changed, she thought, sighing as she looked on each side of her, at her children's heads, bent over their books. *I tried so desperately to believe that one of the many social agencies or civic organizations I contacted would come up with something. I even kept my cell phone until I couldn't pay the bill anymore, hoping someone would call with good news . . . .*

She remembered the day she'd realized her cell phone service had finally been cut off. Now what? How did one of those agencies contact her if something actually did turn up?

All the more reason to check my email, she reminded herself, *and to hope and pray they don't eventually cancel my account. Maybe today there'll be some good news.*

She glanced over at the computer stations, but they were still occupied. She'd have to watch them closely and grab one as soon as it opened up. Until then she was just relieved to be somewhere warm and clean, somewhere her children didn't have to be afraid of "bad people" or strange noises in the night.

Glancing toward the front desk, she smiled at the sight of Louise, stamping and sorting through a pile of books. The familiarity of the sight warmed her heart and encouraged her in a way she didn't understand but greatly appreciated.

❄ ❄ ❄

The skies were still clear as the sun sank toward the Western horizon, and the wind blew more sharply than ever. Josie and the kids shivered as they stood in line with at least 100 others, waiting and hoping for a bed for the night. She'd heard of this particular shelter while she was at the library that afternoon and had quickly loaded her kids on the bus and headed for it. Apparently it didn't open until early December and closed again some time in February or March, but it was one more resource for the next few weeks.

Children, several younger than Susanna, stood beside their parents or slept in their arms, while others cried from the cold. *And maybe from hunger*, Josie thought, grateful she still had enough to feed her own children tonight and in the morning. If they got into the shelter, they'd get a light supper and even breakfast tomorrow, meaning she could save the last of their food for later in the day. After that they might have to take up the Lunds on their offer to drop by for dinner now and then, though that meant spending money on bus fare to get there and then making sure they left to come back downtown before the buses stopped running for the night. *And we'd never make it back in time to get into the shelter.* She frowned at the thought of having to choose between a hot meal for her children or a warm place to sleep.

"Next," someone called.

Josie looked toward the deep male voice that had called out. Only two more families stood between Josie and the elderly man in the wheelchair with the clipboard resting on his lap. He was wrapped in a warm jacket with a blanket over his legs, asking questions and making notes as hopeful people reached his spot in front of the line. Maybe Josie and the kids would make it inside after all.

Within minutes they were standing directly in front of the old man, who smiled up at them. His glasses were thick, and behind them Josie could see his eyes were rheumy. But his welcome was warm, and she felt a spark of hope as she answered his questions.

"Well, Mrs. Meyers," the man said at last, "I believe we have room for you and your children. Please, go on inside. You'll find blankets and pillows in the bin on your left. Just make your way down the aisle to the first available cots. Sandwiches will be served within the hour."

"Do you have donuts for breakfast?" Susanna asked.

The old man chuckled. "Well, if we don't, we should," he said. "But I know we have something for you in the morning, so you just go on inside and get warm."

"What's your name?" Susanna asked.

The man chuckled again. "My name is Mr. Foley. What's yours?"

"I'm Susanna," she answered. "And this is my brother, Jacob."

"Well, I'm mighty glad to meet you both, Susanna and Jacob," he said, extending his hand to Susanna first and then Jacob, clasping it and holding on for several seconds as he looked into their faces. "I'm glad you've joined us tonight."

"Me too," said Susanna. "I don't like the other place with the bad people."

The man's smile faded and his heavy dark eyebrows rose. Before he could respond, Josie pressed her hand against the small of Susanna's back and hustled her and Jacob through the door. "Enough talking," she said, loud enough for the man to hear as they hurried away. "Mr. Foley has work to do. There are other people waiting to get inside too. Come on now. Let's get our blankets and pillows and find our cots for the night."

By the time they'd settled onto the first three empty cots that were side by side, Susanna was complaining about being hungry.

"You heard the man," Josie said. "We'll be getting sandwiches in a little while."

"But I'm hungry now," she whined. "Don't we still have food in your backpack?"

Josie's cheeks flushed, and she hoped no one around them had heard. She leaned forward. "Yes, we do," she whispered, laying a hand on her daughter's shoulder to soften her words. "But we're saving that for tomorrow. While we're here, we'll eat what they serve us, just like everyone else. Understand?"

Her eyes downcast, Susanna nodded.

"All right then," Josie said. "Now just sit here patiently until they announce that it's time to eat."

"Mom?"

Josie looked toward her son, who sat two cots away from Susanna, his brow furrowed. Josie had already laid her belongings on the bed in the middle, so she scooted over to sit on it while Jacob talked to her. "What is it, honey?" she asked.

"Why is Mr. Foley in a wheelchair?"

Josie paused. "I don't know. It could be all sorts of reasons. You've seen people in wheelchairs before. Even your dad . . . " Her voice trailed off and she wished she could call back the words. But of course she couldn't, even as the memory of an emaciated Sam in a wheelchair during the last days of his life filled her mind and pierced her heart.

107

"I know," Jacob said. "That's what I was thinking of . . . Dad." His chin trembled but he continued. "Do you think Mr. Foley has cancer too? Is he going to die?"

The lump in her throat that had plagued her for months now seemed to expand in size and intensity. Oh, how she wished she had some easy answers for her son! Her children were being thrust into the realities of life—and death—far too early.

"He might have cancer," she said at last. "But it could be a lot of other things too. Sometimes older people use wheelchairs just because they're tired or weak."

"Yeah, but . . . is he going to die?"

Josie took a deep breath. "Someday," she said. "Yes, Mr. Foley will die someday. We all will; you know that."

Jacob's jaws twitched. "That's not what I mean. Is he going to die . . . soon?"

Once again tears bit her eyes. "I don't know, son," she said, reaching out to brush a stray lock from his forehead. "I honestly don't know."

"He's old," Susanna said from behind her. "He has to die soon."

Jacob stared at his sister for a moment, but just as Josie told herself she had to end this conversation and move on to something else, a woman standing near the entrance blew a whistle and clapped her hands. When she had everyone's attention she called out, "Volunteers will come around to bring you a sandwich and a cup of water. Just wait on your cots until they arrive. Bathrooms are at the back of the building—women's on the left, men's on the right. Children must be with an adult at all times. Lights out in one hour, and breakfast burritos will be served at seven. Thank you all for joining us tonight."

A buzz began around the room as everyone realized the announcement was complete and food was coming. Josie was relieved. It signaled the end of the conversation about death and the promise of one more safe night. For now, that was the best she could hope for.

*　❄　❄　❄*

It was Susanna who woke her mother in the morning, a definite role reversal that surprised Josie. It was the first really good night's sleep she'd had since leaving the Lunds' place. Cots in a shelter were somehow more welcoming than sleeping in the midst of who knew what sort of crimes going on around them.

"It's almost time for breakfast burritos," Susanna announced, her face just inches from Josie's as she leaned over her bed. "That's almost as good as donuts."

Josie smiled. "You're right about that," she said, pulling herself to a sitting position. Most everyone, including Jacob, was already up by then, packing their things and getting ready to grab some grub on their way out the door. Josie realized she'd better hurry if they were going to be able to use the restrooms before leaving.

Stuffing her things into her backpack, she instructed the children to do the same. "We'll all have to go to the ladies' bathroom first," she said. "Jacob, you wait right by the door while Susanna and I go inside. We won't take long. Then we'll wait by the men's room while you run inside too. OK?"

Jacob shrugged and nodded. Josie knew he was already familiar with the routine and wasn't particularly crazy about it—especially the waiting by the women's bathroom part. But he also knew the rules: kids must stay with parents/adults at all times.

By the time they'd finished their cleanup and bathroom drills, breakfast was being handed out at the door. The burritos were warm, wrapped in foil, and accompanied by small juice containers. Susanna seemed more excited about the juice than the burritos, but Josie was just concerned about where they would eat their food once they got outside.

They stepped through the door, backpacks over their shoulders and food in hand, to a cold, dark day but, at least for now, no rain. Josie was relieved. It made eating outside a lot easier.

"Where are we going today, Mommy?" Susanna asked between bites.

"Louise is working again today," Josie answered, "so we'll go back to the library." She smiled. "And since we saved money by staying here instead of a motel last night, we'll catch the bus so we won't have to walk. How does that sound?"

"It sounds great!" Susanna beamed. "Where does it stop to pick us up?"

"Right out front," Josie answered. "I heard two ladies talking about it in the restroom a little while ago."

110   Susanna took a sip of her juice and then looked around. "Where's Jacob?"

A lightning blast of fear shot up Josie's back, ending in prickles under the skin of her cheeks. Terrified, she turned in all directions, frantically scanning the milling breakfast eaters. How had she let him out of her sight? Where could he have gone?

"Jacob!" Her voice shook as she called his name, her worst nightmare coming into focus. Even before Sam died she had worried if either of her children was out of her sight, but since being homeless her fears had multiplied.

"Jacob," she called again, louder this time.

"I'm over here, Mom," came his voice from a spot back against the wall near the door. "I'm talking to Mr. Foley."

Sure enough, Josie's eyes came to rest on her waving son, standing next to the old man in the wheelchair. Her hammering heart slowed slightly as she grabbed Susanna and steered her in Jacob's direction.

"Don't ever do that to me again, young man," she ordered. "You know we're supposed to stay together, no matter what. You scared me half to death!"

Jacob's cheeks flushed. "I'm sorry, Mom," he said. "I just saw Mr. Foley and wanted to say good-bye before we left. He . . . he was just telling me that I shouldn't wander off by myself."

"That's true," the old man said. "In a perfect world, we wouldn't have to worry about those things. But this old world is far from perfect."

Josie made eye contact with Mr. Foley and sensed his concern was genuine. "Thank you," she said. "He's usually so good about that; both of them are. But he's also very friendly, as you can see. I hope he didn't bother you."

Mr. Foley smiled. "Not at all. He's a nice boy, and I enjoy the company."

"Well," Josie said, "I suppose we'd better get going. We're headed to the library so the kids can study."

Mr. Foley nodded, and Josie knew he realized the library was as much a place to stay warm as a place to study, but he didn't say a word. She liked the old man more all the time.

"We're going to ride the bus," Susanna announced. "We don't have to walk there today."

"Well now," Mr. Foley said, "that sounds like a good idea to me. But I happen to know the bus won't be here for at least twenty minutes, so that means you have time to finish your breakfast first. I hope you'll join me right here in this little spot so we can eat together." He turned to Jacob. "What do you think, Jacob?"

The boy nodded. "I like it," he said. "And I like these burritos too."

They chuckled as they all returned to their breakfasts, which had cooled a bit in the last few moments but still tasted very good to Josie.

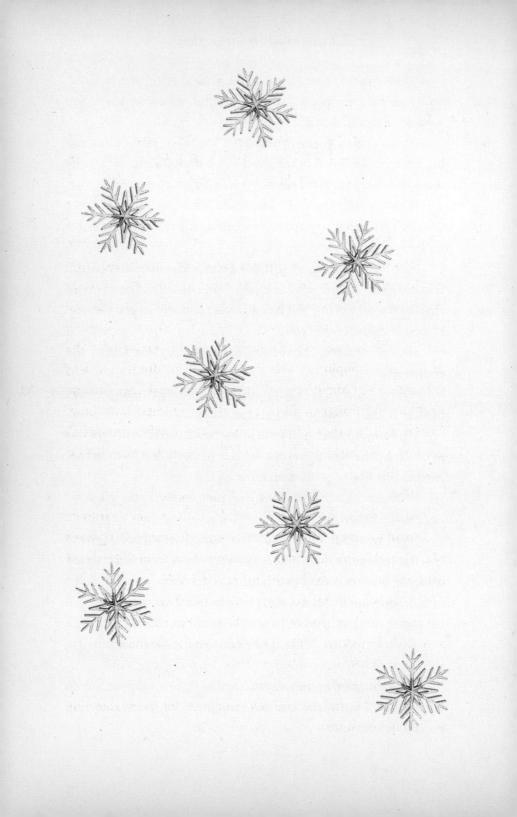

CHAPTER 14

The library was warm and cozy that Wednesday morning, but emptier than usual. As a result Josie imagined she'd be able to check her email and browse the Internet a bit once she got the children settled in with their books. They were all comfortably full from the burritos they'd had at the shelter, and they still had enough sandwiches left for lunch. She considered dropping by the Lunds' place for dinner but was still concerned about not getting back to the shelter in time to get beds that night, and that was the most important thing. The sandwiches they'd been given the night before weren't as good as a hot meal in Arlene Lund's kitchen, but they would have to do.

"Mom?"

Josie stood in front of the children, leaning over to arrange their books and papers on the table nearest the computer stations so she could keep an eye on them while she was online. She raised her head to meet Jacob's gaze. "What is it, honey?"

"Did you know Mr. Foley is homeless too?"

Josie raised her eyebrows. She hadn't even considered it. He seemed to be just one more volunteer, helping the others.

"No, I didn't," she admitted. "How'd you find that out?"

Jacob shrugged. "I asked him."

Josie smiled and nodded. Of course he did. Jacob could be very straightforward when he wanted to be.

"His wife died a few years ago," Jacob said, "and his son lives in Connecticut. He never sees him and only talks to him once in a while. That's kinda sad, don't you think?"

"It sure is," she agreed. "And you learned all this in those few minutes you were talking to Mr. Foley before Susanna and I joined you?"

Jacob nodded. "Yep. When Mr. Foley's wife died he was so sad that he started drinking. Pretty soon he lost his house. He still has a car, but now he doesn't have to sleep in it anymore because the people who run the shelter are his friends and told him he could live there now. He helps them in lots of ways."

Josie forced a smile. Mr. Foley was eighty if he was a day. How tragic must it be for a man his age—and in a wheelchair besides—to have to live in his car! "I'm sure he does," she said, patting her son's hand. "He seems like a very nice man. But now it's time for you to get started on your studies."

She glanced at Susanna, who was already deeply engrossed in her picture book. Placing her finger under her daughter's chin, she tilted the girl's face up to get her attention. "I'm going to be on the computer for a few minutes," she said, indicating with a quick nod where it was located. "I'm right here if you need me. Don't go anywhere—not even to the restroom—without telling me first. Do you understand?"

Her eyes went back and forth from one child to the other. When they had both nodded their understanding, she said, "Good. Let me know when you get hungry. We still have some peanut butter sandwiches for lunch."

Once their heads were again bent down toward their books, she settled into the nearby seat and began to work the mouse and keyboard until she'd brought up her email account. Seventeen messages in her inbox, though most should have landed in the junk folder. She went down the line, deleting those until she came to one from the county. Her heart raced as she imagined a notice telling her they had found transitional housing for her and the children. But as she read through the brief message she realized that wasn't the case at all. In fact, it was a notice that they needed yet another signed form from her regarding that housing. The form had been mailed to her post office box and waited for her there. The sooner they got it back, the better.

She sighed. It hadn't been there when she picked up her December check, and she hadn't bothered to stop by the post office since. *Looks like we'll have to leave the library earlier than I planned so we can swing by there before we go to the shelter. Sure would help if they were at least in the same direction, but now we'll have to catch an extra bus today. But it's just too cold and too far to walk. All the more reason to get to the shelter on time so we don't get stuck spending money on a motel room.*

Josie glanced over at her kids. Except for the overstuffed backpacks crammed under the table where they sat, they appeared to be normal children enjoying a day at the library. Sadly, Josie knew better.

Sensing someone watching her, she moved her gaze from the children toward the front desk. Louise stood at the counter, another stack of books in front of her, as she stared out at Josie. When their eyes met, Louise's cheeks flushed and she waved. Josie appreciated her friendliness, but she couldn't help but wonder what the woman must think of her.

Karen's feet hurt. She'd worked at the church most of the morning, sorting through donations of clothing and other miscellaneous items. As much as she enjoyed volunteering at various places, she was glad she had a few hours between lunch and the midweek service to run a few errands and then zip home for a quick nap before returning to church.

She pulled into the parking lot at a large discount department store, hoping to be able to pick up everything she needed in one spot and avoid any other detours on the way home. Finding a parking place near the entrance, she pulled her hood over her head and opted to leave her umbrella in the car as she hurried inside.

I've been wet before, she told herself with a silent chuckle. *In Washington, what's a few more raindrops?*

Once inside she removed the damp hood from her head and plotted out her route. She'd hit the pharmacy first, then cruise through the beauty section and pick up some shampoo, then on to the grocery aisles at the far left. That should do it, though she'd been known to get sidetracked by a special or two on more than one occasion.

It happened as she made her way toward the groceries.

Prepaid cell phones. On special — two for one. Hmm . . .

She didn't need one for herself, but she knew immediately who did.

Josie and her kids. Definitely. And Rick. It would simplify things so much for all of them. Then again, is it right or fair to purchase phones for them when so many others don't have them?

It was a question she wrestled with often, and always she came back to the same answer. She couldn't do everything for everyone, but she could do a few things for some.

Should I do it, Lord? Is this something You want me to do, or just another one of my emotional impulses?

The warm peace that covered her at that moment sealed it for her. She picked up the two-for-one phones and popped them in her basket before continuing on to get eggs and milk. More than likely she'd see Rick this evening, if he stopped by for a ride to church as he said he would. As far as Josie and her children, she'd just have to pray that God would allow them to cross paths again soon.

* * *

It had been an exhausting day, and Josie had spent more on bus fare than she'd intended, but the detour to the post office required it. She'd retrieved the form and filled it out in the post office before mailing it back, and then they'd caught another bus to the shelter. Now they stood in line once again, hoping for entrance.

Josie could see the door from where they stood, with about ten people in front of them. Mr. Foley sat in his wheelchair, next to the door and under the eaves, protected from the steady mist that soaked the rest of them. Jacob stood stoically in his zippered, hooded jacket and mittens, staring straight ahead. Josie couldn't help but wonder what thoughts and emotions wrestled in his mind.

Susanna, on the other hand, huddled under her mother's embrace, shivering as she pressed up against her. Josie had noticed the child coughing a time or two, and now she sniffled as well. Was she catching a cold? Oh, how she prayed not, but in this weather, it was nearly inevitable.

Please let us get inside tonight, she prayed silently, resenting the need to present such a petition but knowing she had no choice. If only God would listen and respond!

Nearly ten minutes passed before they reached the front door and Mr. Foley. The old man grinned in recognition the moment he looked up and saw them, but Josie thought he looked paler than he had that morning. Perhaps the cold was getting to him as well, though he was bundled up tightly and even had a small blanket across his lap.

"You're back," he said. "I was hoping you'd get here soon enough."

A rush of relief nearly took Josie's breath away. "Does that mean we can get in tonight?" she asked.

Mr. Foley nodded. "You betcha. Just made it, though. The place is filling up fast."

The thought that others would be turned away tore at Josie's heart, but she knew there was nothing to be done about it. She only hoped that none of those left out in the cold included children.

Gratefully she escorted her two little ones inside, basking in the warmth that greeted them the moment they walked through the door. Maybe a good night's sleep would clear up Susanna's sniffles and cough. If not, Josie would have to go to a drugstore and splurge on some medicine first thing in the morning. Of course, she could take advantage of the state's medical plan, since the children were put on it when they applied for aid. But Josie had long ago decided not to avail herself of that particular benefit unless it was a real emergency. She'd heard too many horror stories of children being taken from parents and put in foster care for no other reason than that the family was homeless and had shown up in the ER. The three of them had lost everything else over the past year, but at least they still had each other. Josie intended to make sure that never changed.

As they located three cots together and settled down to await their sandwiches, Josie realized tomorrow's breakfast at the shelter was their last assured meal. They had finished the food the Lunds gave them, and tomorrow Josie would have to buy an inexpensive lunch for the three of them. Should she take a chance after that and go to the Lunds' for dinner, or just come back to the shelter and once again try to get a bed for the night?

She sighed. Never in her life had she imagined expending so much energy trying to decide what should be such simple aspects of life: food and shelter. At this point, their entire existence boiled down to that. Could they hold out until they finally got some sort of public housing?

Susanna sneezed and wiped her nose with her sleeve. Josie pulled a rumpled tissue from her pocket and handed it to her daughter. "Use this, sweetheart," she said, "not your sleeve."

The child looked up at her and nodded. Her eyes were glassy, and Josie sighed. Quite obviously it was going to take more than one good night's sleep to clear up Susanna's problems. They would definitely have to stop at a drugstore on their way to the library in the morning.

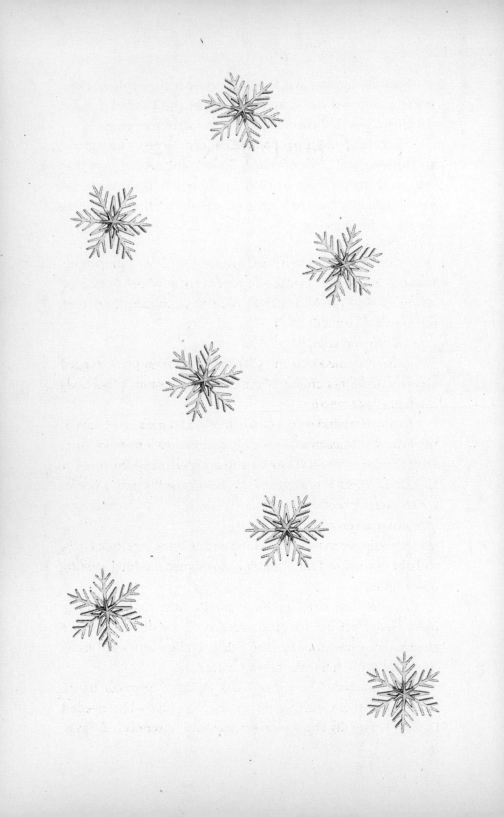

CHAPTER 15

I'm cold, Mommy."

Susanna's voice in her ear yanked Josie from a deep sleep. Instantly awake, she scrambled from her cot and knelt beside her daughter. "Did you kick your blanket off?" she asked, reaching out to recover the child.

"No. I'm just cold."

Josie confirmed that the girl's blanket was in place, tugged securely under her chin. But she could see Susanna's frail body shivering underneath.

Laying her hand on the child's forehead, Josie's heart sank at the heat that impacted her palm. Susanna had a fever for sure. Did Josie dare wait until morning to get some medicine then, or should she break down and ask for help, possibly even a ride to the emergency room?

"I have an extra bottle of water."

The whisper came from behind and above where Josie knelt, and she turned to find a woman in rumpled clothing looking down at her.

"I never can sleep in these places," she said, her long, disheveled, black hair streaked with gray. "But it's better than the streets, so I come anyway." She held a bottle out toward Josie. "Here, take this. It'll make her feel better."

Josie nodded. The woman was right. If Susanna had a fever—and there was no doubt that she did—she needed liquids. Gratefully she took the water and unscrewed the cap.

She had to urge her daughter to drink, but at last she got a few sips down her.

"I'm going to put another blanket on you, Susanna," she said, reaching behind her to pull the cover from her own cot. "That'll make you feel better."

Susanna nodded, and her eyes fluttered shut. After a few moments her breathing became deep and even again, and Josie relaxed. Maybe they could wait until morning after all.

Rising to her feet to return to her now coverless bed, she was surprised to find the lady still standing behind her. "Thank you again for the water," Josie said. "It was very kind of you."

"I had a little girl once." The woman's eyes peered through the semidarkness at Josie, but her focus seemed far away.

Josie raised her eyebrows. "Really? Where is she now?"

Cracks seemed to appear in the woman's face as she blinked back tears. "Gone," she said, her voice somewhere between a sob and a croak. "They took her away."

"Who took her away? What do you mean?"

The woman pointed one finger upward. "Aliens," she answered. "The government said they were going to take her to a foster home because I couldn't take good care of her, but I know that's not true. It was aliens. They took her to another planet to marry their ruler."

The tears that had glistened in the woman's eyes spilled over onto her dry, thin cheeks, and she shook her head as she spoke. "But she was only eight years old. Who gets married when they're eight? She was too young. Too young to go away and get married."

Josie realized she'd been holding her breath, and she exhaled slowly. Quite obviously the woman wasn't playing with a full deck, but how much if anything of what she had said was true? Had she possibly had a daughter once? Had the state taken her away? If so, why? Because the mother was mentally unstable? Or had she become mentally unstable because they took her child away from her? Had the woman become homeless after losing her daughter . . . or had she lost her daughter because they were homeless?

Seeming to return to the present, the woman placed her cold hand on Josie's arm. "The water will help," she said. "I always gave water to my Marcie when she had a fever."

Josie, struggling to find the right words, nodded slowly. "Yes," she said at last. "Water is good for fevers. Thank you so much."

The woman offered a weak smile and turned away, as Josie sank back onto her cot. Unrolling the jacket she'd been using as a pillow, she lay down and covered herself with it as best she could. She prayed Susanna would feel better by morning because, right now, the last thing she wanted to do was take her daughter to a county medical facility.

❄ ❄ ❄

Karen had spent a rare morning sleeping in, surprised when she awoke to sunshine peeking through her bedroom window. Though she knew it was a thin winter sun, it was bright nonetheless, and she sat up in bed with a feeling of anticipation.

"What is it, Father?" she asked. "You have a gift for me today, don't You?"

She felt the smile of response in her heart and stood to her feet, grabbing her robe and sliding her feet into her slippers as she did so. "Let's go have a cup of coffee together, Lord, and You can tell me all about it."

By the time an hour had passed, Karen had spent considerable time reading the Scriptures, praying, and listening for direction. She was grateful she didn't have to be anywhere in particular that day, as she was relatively sure God was going to direct her somewhere specific. Though she hadn't received a direct answer from Him, she had come to the conclusion that it had something to do with Josie and her children, and she imagined her Father was going to do something to connect them all so she could give them the phone she'd bought for them. As planned, she'd been able to deliver a phone to Rick when he stopped by for a ride to church the previous evening, and she'd asked God to provide a way for her to get Josie's to her as well.

Showered and dressed at last, she climbed into her car, more certain than ever that God had a mission for her that day. Continuing to listen as she backed out of the driveway, she suddenly pictured the entrance to the library and knew that's where she was to go.

Parking in the lot, she climbed from her car, turning her face upward. *Thank You for the sunshine, Lord,* she prayed silently. *May I spread some of it to Josie and her little ones, as well as anyone else I meet this day!*

She'd no sooner stepped through the front doors when she spotted the little threesome huddled at a back table. Jacob's head was bent over a book, while Josie seemed to be whispering to Susanna, touching the girl's forehead and appearing quite concerned. The child was bundled in a warm parka-type jacket, though the room was toasty warm.

Karen frowned with concern and approached the family, who seemed not to notice her until she was nearly in front of them. Josie spotted her first, her eyes widening for a brief moment before her cheeks turned a faint pink. The smile that followed was stiff.

"Hello," Josie said, her voice quiet as she nodded.

Karen smiled, remembering her determination to spread sunshine and silently asking God to help her do so. "Hello to you," she said, watching as both children lifted their heads and spotted her. Jacob registered recognition immediately, but Susanna's stare was glassy and vague.

"How are you all doing?" Karen asked, continuing to smile.

Josie hesitated before she shrugged. "Oh, OK, I guess. And you?"

"I'm fine," Karen answered. "But Susanna's not looking too well." She turned her gaze toward the girl. "Are you not feeling too well today, sweetheart?"

Susanna shook her head slowly from side to side. "I'm sick," she said. "I want to go to bed."

The child's words pierced Karen's heart, as she realized how nearly impossible it was for a homeless mother to put her children to bed during the day.

"Hush," Josie said, stroking Susanna's hair. "We'll get you to bed soon, I promise. Just as soon as we can check into a motel, I promise."

"Ridiculous," Karen said, not meaning to sound so sharp. "You'll do no such thing. I told you my home is open to you until you can find something else. And even if you're not willing to take me up on it normally, surely you can see the need to do so now for Susanna's sake. This is no time for false pride, Josie Meyers. Your daughter is sick."

The slight pink in Josie's cheeks turned to flaming red, and Karen saw the flash of anger in the woman's eyes before they filled with tears and her shoulders slumped.

"I know," she whispered. "I thought about you this morning but didn't know how to reach you. We've been staying at a shelter at night, but as you know, we have to leave during the day. I decided to spend some money on a motel today because we can check in earlier there than at the shelter, but — "

"I hate motels," Susanna interrupted. "Bad people stay there."

Karen raised her eyebrows. She could only imagine what sort of rooms the family had been forced to rent in order to stretch their meager income. Well, no more of that.

Karen reached down and began to gather up the books and papers scattered across the table. "Enough talk," she said. "Let's pack up everything and head to my place. You can stay through the holidays if you like, or at least until Susanna is feeling better."

Josie's protest was feeble. "But we can't impose. We—"

Karen held up her hand. "I'm not listening. Right now we're going to climb into my car and go home. I left a pot of soup bubbling in the Crock-Pot, and it should just about be ready when we get there."

She spotted the first sign of a smile on Susanna's face, and her heart warmed. *Keep shining, Lord*, she prayed silently. *These precious people need Your light.*

As they walked toward the door, Karen noticed the librarian watching them with a smile. Karen returned the smile and then reached into her purse and pulled out the phone she'd tucked into the side pocket. "This is for you," she said, handing it to Josie. "I got it yesterday. There's enough time on it for emergencies, so use it wisely. I don't want you being without a source of communication. You need that for your children."

Once again Josie's blue eyes pooled with tears, but she took the phone without protest as the four of them stepped outside into the noonday sun.

Karen smiled as she glanced up. "Thank You, Father," she whispered as they headed to the car.

"Amen," Susanna said softly, and Karen's heart sang.

❄ ❄ ❄

By evening Josie felt the tightness around her chest begin to release. Susanna's fever was down, she wasn't coughing nearly as much, and she was sleeping soundly in the double bed in Karen's spare room. Josie would sleep beside her tonight, while Jacob curled up on the living room couch. It was the most secure Josie had felt since they were staying with the Lunds, but the way that situation had turned out prevented her from truly relaxing in her new surroundings.

After all, it's just temporary, she reminded herself, as she stood over the bed staring down at her sleeping daughter. *Even if I decide to take Karen up on her offer to stay through the holidays, we still have to go back out there sooner or later. How much longer can we keep going on like this?*

She thought then of her desperation as the three of them had sat in the library that morning. Even with the baby aspirin and cough medicine she'd picked up at the store, Susanna had still shivered and coughed and whined about wanting to go to bed. Josie had decided then that she had no choice but to rent a cheap motel room until Susanna felt better. Nights at the shelter just weren't enough, and there was always the chance they might arrive too late for a bed and they'd have to go to a motel anyway . . . or try the alley behind the cleaners again.

She shuddered at the thought, even as she realized they hadn't been back to that spot since Thanksgiving evening, when Rick had come to take them to the warehouse that had opened its doors for the night. She knew Jacob would remind her that God had answered his prayer to give them a warm place to sleep, but she still resisted the idea that the Almighty was looking out for them in any way. If He were, why would He have let them lose their home in the first place? If He truly was so all-knowing and all-powerful — not to mention all-loving — why hadn't He stepped in earlier and prevented the many tragedies that had demolished their lives?

She shook her head. No, she wasn't buying into that loving God stuff. She was grateful Karen had come to their rescue, just as the Lunds and Rick had done earlier. But it was all just coincidence, nothing more.

Then why do you pray?

The thought seemed to have come out of nowhere, but it snagged her attention and wouldn't let go. Why did she pray, indeed, if she didn't think there was at least a chance God would hear and answer?

She blinked away the tears and turned from the bed, telling herself she needed to go into the other room and check on Jacob. But the question followed her out the door.

CHAPTER 16

Rick had basked in the sunlight of the crisp winter day, despite the coughing that seemed to be on the increase. The accompanying pain and spitting up of blood told him he was getting worse, but he'd already assumed as much. His time was getting close, and he had already made peace with that. In fact, he found himself longing for it more each day.

But the pale yellow orb had sunk behind the horizon now, leaving a dark, cloudless sky that sparkled with stars but forced temperatures below freezing in a matter of hours. He'd tried to get into a couple of shelters but had opted to give up his bed in one for an elderly woman who showed up late. By the time he arrived at the second place, it was full.

His pace slower than what it was just a few days earlier, he plowed his way down the nearly deserted streets, hunched against the cold with his jacket pulled tight. He thought of the cell phone in his pocket, tempted to call Karen and ask if he could possibly spend the night on her back porch or even in her car, but he thought better of it. It wasn't right to put her in such a position, knowing how many homeless people she helped on a regular basis and that she couldn't possibly house all of them.

He thought then of the little family he'd first met on Thanksgiving and wondered where they were staying now. He'd heard they were no longer with the Lunds and had been spending time at the shelter he had gone to first this evening, but he hadn't seen them there. He just prayed they were somewhere off the streets.

"Please, Lord," he whispered, choking back a cough, "keep them safe and well. It's one thing for me to be out here, but not them, Lord. Not them."

He arrived at his destination, pleased to find the alley behind the cleaners empty. Ever since finding Josie and her children there, he had made it a regular stopping place for himself at night when nothing else was available. So far no one else had challenged him to the spot, and he figured it was about as good as it got for sleeping outdoors.

"Thanks for providing this place, Lord," he said as he settled in against the wall under the overhang. At least it wasn't raining, but oh, was the air cold! He pulled his jacket tighter and wrapped a thin blanket around his shoulders. It was going to be a long night.

* * *

Both children were asleep and Josie was about to bed down herself when she heard a light rap on the bedroom door.

"Josie?" The voice was just above a whisper. "Are you awake?"

Already sitting on the edge of the bed next to her sleeping child, Josie considered not answering. Would Karen go away if she remained quiet?

"Josie?"

She sighed. Apparently not. Besides, it wouldn't be right. She owed Karen — big time. Being homeless didn't give her an excuse to be rude or ungrateful.

"Just a minute," she called softly, grabbing the robe she'd just removed. "I'll be right out."

A moment later she joined her host in the kitchen.

"How about a cup of decaf?" Karen asked, her round face pleasant as she stood by the stove where a kettle boiled. "Or I have tea if you prefer."

"Decaf is fine," Josie said. "Anything really. Whatever you're having."

Karen snagged a couple of mugs from the cupboard and dropped a decaf bag in each, then filled them with boiling water. "Cream or sugar?"

Josie shook her head. "Black is fine."

They sat down at the small round table in the corner, their steaming mugs in front of them. Josie waited, wondering what to say or do next. Conversation had revolved around the children most of the afternoon and evening, but now it was just the two of them.

"How about a cookie with that?" Karen asked, her eyes twinkling. "I shouldn't have one, especially since we had ice cream after dinner, but if you say yes I'll have an excuse to join you."

131

Josie chuckled in spite of herself. "Sure," she said. "I must admit to being a bit of a cookie freak myself."

Sharing decaf and cookies made it easier to relax as they sat together at the table, and soon they were talking about everything from favorite flowers to recipes. Josie even broke down and shared a bit about the last couple years of her life.

"What I miss more than anything," Josie said, the remnants of her cookie on a plate in front of her, "is my kitchen. It was big and sunny and . . . "

Her voice trailed off as she fought tears. "I'm sorry," she said. "I don't mean to dwell on the past and all we've lost, but . . . "

Karen laid her hand on Josie's. "You have nothing to apologize for," she said. "Of course you miss your home—and your husband and mother too. You've been through a terrible time the last couple of years. I can't even imagine."

Josie nodded. "True. But I'm not the only one who's lost something . . . or someone. You . . . your husband died, too, didn't he?"

Karen's smile faded. "Yes. Years ago. We were young, with so many dreams." She took a deep breath and her smile returned. "But God had other plans, and His are always greater than our own. He's been a faithful Husband and Provider for me ever since." She squeezed Josie's hand. "I've really had a wonderful and blessed life."

Resisting the impulse to pull her hand away, Josie swallowed the lump in her throat and blinked away the tears that seemed to threaten her nearly all the time these days. She wanted to believe Karen, and maybe it was true for her. But Josie's life was different. It wasn't just that she'd lost her mother and then her husband; it was that she'd discovered Sam wasn't the man she thought he was all along—as if she'd lost him before he ever died. The betrayal was almost worse than the death.

She dropped her eyes and sipped her decaf, hoping to end the conversation and head for bed soon. How much longer would she need to stay before graciously excusing herself? "I'm so glad God led me to you today," Karen said. "I was praying to find you so I could give you that phone."

Josie looked up. "And I appreciate it more than I can say," she answered. "Not to mention offering us a place to stay. I really didn't want to impose, but . . . well, with Susanna being sick . . . "

"Of course," Karen said. "We couldn't let you stay in shelters at night and outside during the day with her feeling like that. And even those cheap motels aren't much better."

"Susanna hates motels," Josie said.

"I heard her say that. I'm so glad you're here instead."

Tears bit her eyes again, but Josie refused to let them win. "I . . . I would have taken her to an emergency room if she'd gotten any worse."

"I know you would have," Karen said.

Feeling the need to defend herself, Josie added, "The only reason I didn't take her today is . . . I . . . I'm afraid." Her voice dropped on the last words, as did her eyes. Did she dare confess her greatest fears to this woman she scarcely knew?

Karen's hand was back on hers, and Josie raised her eyes. The sincerity in Karen's face won her over.

"There was a woman at the shelter last night," she said, speaking just above a whisper. "She offered a bottle of water to Susanna when she realized she had a fever. Then she . . . she said something about her child being . . . taken from her. She said the county told her they were putting her in foster care, but the woman didn't believe them. She said . . . " Josie swallowed and took a deep breath. Would Karen think she was as mentally unstable as the woman at the shelter? "She said her daughter was taken by aliens in a space ship . . . to be married to their leader."

A look of deep sadness washed over Karen's face, and she nodded. "I know who you mean," she said, shaking her head. "Her name is Jenny. Poor thing. And yes, she did lose her daughter to foster care. Jenny is schizophrenic and seldom takes her meds. She and her daughter ended up living on the streets, and eventually the county removed the girl. I imagine it was for the best, but it was devastating for Jenny. She may be mentally unstable, but she truly loved her child—and her child loved her."

133

Josie's insides seemed to twist into a knot. She'd been right not to take Susanna to the emergency room. With all she'd been through in the last couple of years, nothing would compare to losing her children.

"I understand why you didn't take Susanna to emergency," Karen said. "But I also know you would have done it if she got worse and you had no choice." She leaned toward her. "You're a good mom, Josie Meyers. Don't ever let anyone tell you differently."

✳ ✳ ✳

Friday morning dawned icy and clear. Rick shivered under his thin blanket and watched the sky turn from black to purple to blue. At least the clouds hadn't moved in overnight, so it would be dry today.

He gathered up his meager belongings, scratched his beard, and stretched. The final movement seemed to trigger a coughing spell that weakened him so severely he had to sit back down until it passed. At last feeling strong enough to get up and walk to the nearest shelter in hopes of breakfast, he made his way from behind the cleaners and out onto the street, which was still nearly deserted. It was a bit early for most people to arrive at work yet, but he knew he needed to get going before the sun was all the way up or he'd miss out on breakfast.

I need it this morning, Lord, he prayed. *I'm getting weaker, but I've still got a couple of things to do before I'm done here. You know about that appointment I have to keep today, Father, so please help me to get everything done and in place before I come home to You.*

He smiled at the thought. Home at last! What a wonderful thing to look forward to, making these last difficult days worth every moment. Sometimes he got so excited at the prospect that he could hardly keep from dancing with joy.

Of course, I can't, he reminded himself. *It's getting tough just to walk, let alone dance. But one day soon, I'll be dancing with the Savior.*

He grinned. "Thank You, Father," he whispered. "You have blessed me more than I could ever have imagined or hoped—and certainly more than any man could ever deserve."

CHAPTER 17

Josie and the children had stayed at Karen's place throughout the day Friday, with Susanna showing slight improvement by bedtime. When Josie awoke on Saturday morning and realized she'd slept straight through, she quickly laid her hand on her daughter's forehead, alarmed that the girl hadn't awakened her during the night.

Cool. Her forehead is cool!

Josie nearly spoke the words aloud but didn't want to disturb the still sleeping child. After all, the faint light in the room told her daylight hadn't quite broken upon them yet.

But it's coming, she thought, smiling. *Daylight is coming, and my sweet baby is getting better. Thank You, Lord!*

She gasped at the realization of what she'd heard in her mind, even more surprised at the heartfelt enthusiasm behind it.

It's just because my daughter is doing better, she reasoned. *Of course I'm grateful! And that most likely would have happened with or without God's help.*

A pang of guilt stabbed her heart then, and she knew she couldn't dismiss her gratitude so cavalierly. *I know You helped, God,* she said. *And I appreciate it — not just in helping Susanna get better, but in leading Karen to come and find us and invite us here, and even to give us a cell phone.*

The realization that she now had communication for emergencies widened the smile already tugging at her lips. Even if they had to go back out onto the streets today, at least she'd have a way of calling for help if they needed it. It amazed her to realize how much she had come to appreciate the things that once seemed so mundane and commonplace to her.

She lay back down on her pillow, breathing a sigh of relief that the current emergency with Susanna seemed to have passed. Karen had encouraged them to stay through the entire month, which she knew they wouldn't do. But a couple more days couldn't hurt . . . could they? The bed felt luxurious, and the knowledge that her children were safe lulled her back to sleep within minutes.

* * *

"We're going to do something special today," Karen announced as the four of them sat at the table eating a lunch of soup and sandwiches. Josie had worried that the chicken salad sandwiches might be too much for Susanna, but the child was dunking hers in her soup and munching happily. The moment she'd heard Karen's announcement, however, she laid her sandwich on the plate, and her blue eyes danced.

"What?" she asked. "What are we going to do, Miss Karen?"

Karen smiled in response. "We're going to put up the Christmas decorations that I should have put up after Thanksgiving. I just got so busy that I didn't get around to it, but now I see that God has sent me an entire family of helpers, so we're going to make this a group effort. What do you think?"

Susanna beamed. "I think that's great! Where's the tree?"

Karen laughed. "I actually went out and got one this morning. It's in the trunk of my car." She turned to Jacob. "I may need your help bringing it into the house. It's not a real big tree; in fact, I'm surprised I found such a nice one of any size so close to Christmas. But between us, I think we can get it inside and set it up, don't you?"

It was Jacob's turn to beam, and Josie's heart warmed at Karen's wisdom in appealing to the boy's strength. If there was anything Jacob responded to well, it was a reference to his being the "man" in any given situation and, therefore, needed. The very thought threatened Josie's eyes with tears, both as she remembered Christmases past when their family was still together in their own home but also as she relished the thought of the three of them being involved in doing something as normal and fun as decorating Karen's home.

"Thank you," she said, catching Karen's eye.

"It's my pleasure," Karen answered. "In fact, I'm the one who should thank all of you. I think the reason I've been putting off all this decorating stuff is that it's just too much work for one person. But a team of four? Why, we should have it done in no time."

Her eyes twinkled then as she lowered her voice to a conspiratorial tone. "And if we're done by dinnertime, we just might spend the evening making Christmas cookies."

"Yay!" Susanna nearly exploded out of her chair as she clapped her hands and jumped to her feet. "I love Christmas cookies!"

Karen laughed again, and then patted her stomach. "So do I," she said. "Can't you tell?"

Even Josie laughed at that, but then reached out to Susanna and laid her hand on her arm. "This is all wonderful," she said, "but you need to calm down a bit, young lady. You're still getting over being sick, remember?"

The girl's enthusiasm dampened only slightly. "I know, Mommy. But I feel good now."

"I'm sure you do," Josie said. "But let's not take any chances, all right?"

Susanna nodded and sat back down, but the glow remained on her face.

137

"If it's all right with everyone else," Karen said, "I have a plan that should help with that very thing."

All eyes fixed on her as they waited.

"Every team project needs a supervisor, right?"

They all nodded.

"Well, now," Karen said, "I've been thinking that Susanna should be our supervisor. Jacob and I will bring the tree in and get it into the stand. We'll set it in the front room by the window so everyone can see it outside." She looked straight at Susanna then. "That means you can lie on the couch and watch the rest of us as we decorate. You can tell us which decorations to put where, and if we've missed a spot or there's a light out or we need more tinsel. What do you think?"

Susanna's eyebrows raised. "I'd be in charge? Really?"

"Really," Karen said.

Josie saw a flash of doubt cross Jacob's face, but he didn't say a word.

Within moments Karen had snagged the boy and taken him outside to unload the tree, while Josie cleared the table and then got Susanna settled onto the couch. It was one of the most joyful moments she and her children had experienced in what seemed a very long time.

❄ ❄ ❄

Jacob was up early on Sunday, leaving his bed on the couch to come into the spare room where Susanna still slept and Josie lay in bed, contemplating getting up. She had been wondering at the wisdom of going to church with Karen that morning. Susanna did seem much improved, but enough for an outing in the cold weather? Josie didn't think so.

As she watched her son step through the door and into the room, she smiled, remembering his many efforts to shoulder the physical work needed to get the tree up the day before. Comparing that to his now tousled hair and sleepy eyes, not to mention his rumpled clothes, her heart ached with a mixture of pride and protectiveness. She knew her boy would one day become a man, and he already struggled and strained in the early stages of that transition, but she really wasn't ready for it to happen anytime soon.

She held her arms out to him, and he came to her silently, sitting down on the edge of the bed.

"I want to go to church today," he said simply. "Can I?"

Josie felt her eyes widen. Apparently their thoughts had been running along similar channels. She was surprised to realize she wanted to go, too, but she truly did feel it was better to keep Susanna home for another day or so. She wanted to be sure the child was completely well before they left the comfort and hospitality of Karen's home to go back to the shelters and motels.

"We'll have to talk to Miss Karen," she whispered, "and make sure she doesn't mind taking you along, even if Susanna and I stay here."

"I already asked her, and she said OK."

Josie suppressed a chuckle. Her no-nonsense son had planned his strategy before ever coming in to talk to her. "Well, then," she said, continuing to keep her voice down so Susanna could sleep, "I guess there's no reason for you not to go, is there?"

A grin spread across Jacob's face and he nodded. "Good," he said. "Rick's probably coming too."

Josie raised her eyebrows. "He is? How do you know that?"

"Because Miss Karen told me he usually comes over before church and gets a ride with her."

"I see." She smiled. "I know you'll enjoy seeing him again, won't you?"

Jacob nodded. "Yep. I like Rick."

Josie reached up and smoothed his hair. "I know you do, son." Rising to a sitting position, she pulled him into her arms. "I love you, Jacob."

She felt the boy nod again before a sound from the kitchen caught his attention and he pulled away.

"It's almost breakfast time," he said. "I'm going to go take a shower and get dressed before we eat."

"Good idea," Josie agreed, releasing him to turn and grab some clothes from the pile in the corner of the room before he scampered back out the door.

CHAPTER 18

Rick worked hard at keeping his cough under control, not wanting to alarm Jacob. He had been pleasantly surprised when he showed up on Karen's doorstep that morning, looking for a ride, to learn that Josie and her kids were staying there and that Jacob would be accompanying them to church. Rick insisted on sitting in the back seat, directly behind Karen, so Jacob could ride shotgun. From his vantage point, he watched the dark-haired boy staring straight ahead.

"I'm really glad you decided to come with us this morning, Jacob," Rick ventured.

The boy's head turned back in his direction, and a smile spread across his face. "Me too," he said. "I wanted to come even before I knew you'd be here, but it's even better now."

Rick's heart warmed. God had indeed made a special connection between him and this little family, and he was so relieved to know they weren't back out on the streets right now. The weather reports called for a real cold snap in the next few days. Rick wasn't looking forward to it, but knowing how short his time was, he'd rather be out in it himself than to think of a woman and children trying to survive under such conditions.

He dismissed the nagging thought that other families would no doubt be subject to the frigid temperatures and instead returned Jacob's smile. "Thanks," he said. "I'm glad you remembered me. I enjoyed sharing Thanksgiving dinner with you."

Jacob nodded. "Not only that, you kept us from sleeping behind the cleaners that night." The smile faded. "I don't like it back there, but it's better than some places."

Rick's heart constricted at the truth of the boy's statement. How well he knew! Best to change the subject.

"Well, at least now you're staying with Miss Karen," he said. "I'd heard you weren't with the Lunds anymore."

"Yeah," Jacob said, a flicker of sadness crossing his face. "I liked it there, but we couldn't stay. They invited us to come back over for dinner whenever we want, but Mom says it's too hard to get over there on the bus and then make it back to the shelter on time."

"Well, now you don't have to worry about that," Karen chimed in. "If you'd like to go to the Lunds' for dinner one of these evenings, I'd be happy to give you a ride over and then pick you up and bring you back to my place when you're done."

Jacob's face lit up again, as he turned his face toward the driver's side of the car. "Really? You'd do that?"

Karen chuckled. "Of course I would. Friends are important, and I wouldn't want you to lose touch with the Lunds. They're friends of mine, too, you know."

"Maybe you could just come with us and stay for dinner too—all of us together," Jacob suggested.

"Maybe so," Karen agreed. "So long as you all are staying at my place, it really shouldn't be a problem."

Rick watched Jacob's shoulders slump and his head droop then. "I don't know how long that will be," he said. "Mom keeps telling us not to get too comfortable at your house. We love it there, but she says she doesn't want us to go through what happened at the Lunds' all over again. I think . . . " He paused, and Rick knew he was struggling to maintain his composure. "I think she wants to leave as soon as she's sure Susanna's all better."

Karen hesitated before answering, and Rick heard the disappointment in her voice. "I understand," she said. "And we have to honor your mom's wishes. But I'm going to pray she'll decide to stay a little longer."

"Me too," Jacob said, lifting his head, his chin jutting out in determination. "I'm going to pray that at church today."

The cough Rick had been suppressing burst loose then, and he grabbed a handkerchief from his pocket. Time was running out . . . for all of them. He sure was glad to know that God was never late.

✳ ✳ ✳

The Lund family had just entered the church doors when Arlene spotted her friend Karen sitting in a row toward the back. Next to her was a bearded man she'd come to know as Rick, a homeless Vietnam vet who regularly attended their church and recently seemed to have been riding with Karen. But it was the dark-haired child sitting between them that caught Arlene's eye.

She nudged her husband. "Jerry, look. Jacob's here—with Karen."

Her husband steered his gaze in the direction Arlene had indicated with a nod, and his pale blue eyes lit up in recognition. "Jacob," he said. "I've missed the little guy." He frowned then. "I wonder where the rest of the family is."

"Let's go find out," Arlene said.

As Melody and Todd peeled off to find their friends, Arlene and Jerry sidled into the pew where Karen and the others sat, seemingly intent on studying their bulletins while waiting for the service to start. Jacob was the first to spot them.

"Mr. and Mrs. Lund!" He jumped from his seat and threw his arms around Jerry, who stood closest to him. "You're here! I was hoping I'd see you."

As Karen and Rick scooted down, making room for the new arrivals, Jacob resettled himself between Rick and Jerry, with Arlene on the other side of her husband. She quickly reached across her husband to give Jacob a quick hug, which he returned enthusiastically.

"This is a wonderful surprise," she said. "We sure have missed you at our place."

"I've missed you too," Jacob said, his dark eyes dancing. "We were just talking about coming to your house for dinner."

Karen leaned across the others to address Arlene. "Josie's been concerned about coming over on the bus and not making it back to the shelter on time, but I told Jacob I'd be happy to drive them over and pick them up any time you'd like them to come."

"Oh, don't be silly," Arlene said. "If you bring them over for dinner, you have to stay yourself. It would be fun."

She caught sight of Rick then, quietly observing the scene. "And you too," she said. "We'd love to have you join us."

The unassuming man nodded. "I'd be honored," he mumbled before returning his eyes to the bulletin he still held in his lap.

"Good morning," came the call from the pulpit. "Won't you all stand with us to sing our opening songs?"

Arlene turned her attention to the front as Jacob settled in between the two men in their little group. She hadn't realized how very much she'd missed Josie and her children until now. Why wasn't the rest of the family here? She'd have to pull Karen aside and talk to her later, without Jacob around. She certainly hoped everything was all right.

Meanwhile, it was time to focus on their reason for being here. What a faithful God they served, and Arlene so appreciated their times of corporate worship. Having Jacob join them this day was indeed a bonus.

144

＊ ＊ ＊

On Rick's request, Karen dropped him off at a shelter downtown and then headed home with Jacob. Both she and the boy had urged Rick to join them for lunch, but he'd declined, saying he had "other plans."

What sort of plans does a homeless person have? Karen wondered as she pulled into her driveway. She couldn't help but wonder if he'd declined because of his failing health.

Before she could wonder anymore, Jacob opened the passenger door and stepped out. "I'm starved," he announced.

Karen laughed. "So am I," she said. "Let's go see about making some sandwiches, shall we?"

"And cookies for dessert?"

She laughed again and tousled Jacob's hair. "And cookies for dessert," she said, heading up the walkway toward the front door. "We have piles of them from last night, so we may as well get busy eating them. Can't let them go to waste, can we?"

Jacob shook his head. "Nope. But I'm glad you gave some to Rick this morning. I just wish he would have come over and had lunch with us."

"I do too," Karen admitted. "But Rick is a very private man. He's kind and friendly, but he seems to like being on his own most of the time."

Jacob shrugged. "I guess," he admitted.

The front door opened before Karen could turn the handle, and she smiled at the cheerful face of the blonde girl gazing up at her. "Mommy and I made lunch," she announced. "Tuna and peanut butter sandwiches."

"Together?" Jacob said. "Yuck!"

The look of disgust on Susanna's face brought another chuckle to Karen. "Not together," she said. "We made two kinds of sandwiches so everybody could choose." Her eyes darted beyond Karen and Jacob then, out to the driveway. "Where's Rick?"

"He didn't come with us," Jacob answered. "He had something to do, so we left him at one of the shelters."

Susanna's dancing eyes faded to flat, and her smile disappeared. "But we made enough for him too," she said.

"I'm sure you did," Karen said, pulling the girl into a hug as they all stepped into the house. "And I'm sure he would have loved them. But he just couldn't make it this time. But hey, you've got us, and Jacob just told me he's starved. So let's get to work on those sandwiches, shall we?"

Susanna perked up again and turned toward the kitchen. "They're here, Mommy," she said, leading the way.

Jacob was right behind his sister, with Karen bringing up the rear. With or without Rick, it was going to be a nice lunch. She just wished she knew how soon Josie planned to take her children and head back out onto the streets.

CHAPTER 19

Rick sat outside in what was left of the morning's sunshine, watching the clouds drift in and praying they wouldn't bring snow with them. They were no doubt full of precipitation, but it all depended on how low the temperature dropped over the next few nights whether or not that precipitation would be frozen.

Gathered together with about fifty others in the courtyard of the shelter, he shivered. Munching bologna sandwiches, he was grateful that, unlike the rest of the week, the shelter served lunch. The wind was definitely colder than when they'd gone to church that morning.

Church. His mind drifted back to the service. The pastor's teaching out of Luke had been a fresh and insightful look into the coming Christmas story, one Rick never tired of hearing. The praise and worship had been sprinkled with Christmas carols, and the colorful wreaths and poinsettias scattered throughout the sanctuary had made the setting especially cheerful.

But it was the time spent with Jacob that meant the most to him at this particular moment. Rick knew that somewhere he too had a son, though he hadn't seen him since he was a baby. The child's mother had married someone else when Rick foolishly signed away his parental rights, glad to get out of paying child support. It was a decision he had regretted ever since but had learned to live with, knowing his son was undoubtedly better off calling someone else "Dad."

He blinked back tears, determined not to let his regrets get the best of him. Only a couple of years after giving up his son, Rick had come to the Lord, broken and desperately in need of forgiveness. God had graciously poured it out on him, and despite the ongoing pain of his life circumstances, Rick had learned to walk in joyful fellowship with his Savior. But that didn't mean things had been easy.

You've been so faithful, Lord, he prayed silently. *Even when I wasn't—which was an awful lot of the time. I can't thank You enough for that. I know I don't deserve Your love or forgiveness, but I surely do appreciate it. And Father, I really am grateful that You've shown me a way to help that little family. I may not be able to do anything for my own son, but I know he's safe in Your care, wherever he is, so I thank You for bringing Jacob and his family into my life. Bless them, Father. Hold them close and help them, Lord. Please.*

Despite the chill, Rick felt warm from the inside out, and he smiled. Even his dry bologna sandwich tasted better. On top of that, he hadn't coughed in an hour or so. It really was a good day after all.

* * *

By Tuesday evening, Josie knew for certain that Susanna was over whatever cold or infection she'd had, and she could no longer convince herself that she and the children needed to stay at Karen's for that reason. And yet the weather had turned nasty, with a cold front blowing through that left ice and even a small layer of snow in its wake. It was unusual for the Pacific Northwest, but certainly not unheard of. The kids had begged her to let them play outside, and she'd relented and allowed them to do so for a half-hour but had then yanked them back inside to thaw out. She couldn't chance letting Susanna get sick again.

When the temperatures rose, even slightly, she knew she would have to pack up her children and leave.

She lay in bed now, next to her sleeping daughter, listening to the wind howl outside and imagining the snowflakes brushing against the window. There hadn't been enough accumulation for the kids to build much of a snowman that afternoon, but they'd tried and had a blast in the process.

Hot tears stung her eyes at the realization that it took a near-stranger's kindness to afford her children such an enjoyable activity as playing in the snow. Thanks to Karen, Jacob and Susanna could bundle up and head outside to frolic as they had before their world caved in. Josie could allow them to do so because she knew she could bring them back into a cozy, dry house when they were through, where they would eat a hot meal and sleep in a warm bed. But for how much longer?

She turned her head to gaze at her daughter, sleeping peacefully beside her. Jacob, too, was no doubt in dreamland, cuddled up on the couch in the front room. A part of Josie longed to accept Karen's gracious invitation to stay at least through the holidays, perhaps even until she reached the top of the list for subsidized housing. But in reality, who knew how long that would take? Days, weeks . . . months? They simply couldn't live here with Karen indefinitely. And another heartbreak, like the one her children had experienced as a result of the demands of the Lunds' landlord, was something Josie wasn't willing to allow Jacob or Susanna to experience.

Or myself, she thought. *The longer we stay here, the more it will begin to seem like home and the harder it will be to leave. No, we need to leave as soon as the weather improves a little. I've got enough money to keep us fed and in cheap motels through the end of the month, especially if we can get into shelters most of the time. I'll worry about January when it gets here.*

149

With that resolution in mind, she closed her eyes and allowed her thoughts to return to a time before her dreams had turned to nightmares.

❄ ❄ ❄

Josie had broken down and gone to Wednesday night service with Karen, and despite her misgivings, had enjoyed the more informal atmosphere and in-depth study. Jacob and Susanna had raved about the children's program and badgered her about taking them back the next week. Josie had hedged on her answer, unwilling to make a commitment she wasn't sure she could keep. After all, by the coming week, she was relatively sure they would no longer be staying at Karen's house.

But for now, they were still there, riding out the exceptionally cold weather. It was Thursday afternoon, and Karen was out attending to one of her many volunteer activities. Josie had supervised the children's studies for most of the day, but now they were getting ready for an evening outing.

"I can't wait to go to the Lunds' tonight," Susanna exclaimed, perhaps for the third or fourth time since learning of their plans. "Is it time yet?"

Josie smiled and pulled her daughter into an embrace. Susanna didn't stay put long. The two of them were in the spare room, as Susanna changed into her clean outfit. Josie thought it might be good while they were there that evening to look through some of the belongings they'd left with Arlene to see if they should switch out some of their existing clothes for something different.

Oh, how Josie wished they could keep all their belongings with them! They didn't have much, but it was difficult leaving even a few sacks or boxes behind, though she so appreciated the Lunds for allowing them to do so.

"Mommy," Susanna pressed, "you didn't answer me. Is it time to go yet?"

Josie pulled her thoughts back to her little girl, standing in front of her with rosy cheeks and clear eyes. How grateful she was for her child's restored health!

She managed to plant a kiss on Susanna's forehead before she wriggled away. "Not quite yet," Josie said, "but soon. By the time you get changed, Miss Karen should be home. Then we'll all head over there together."

Susanna grinned. "I'm glad Miss Karen is going to stay and eat with us." She clapped her hands together and exclaimed, "It'll be like a party!"

Josie laughed. "It certainly will, won't it? Now get dressed. I want to brush your hair before we go."

"Will you put my pink barrettes in it?"

"Of course I will," Josie said, marveling that with all they'd lost, the child had somehow managed to hang on to her favorite barrettes, a pair Josie's mother had bought for her just before she died. "You'll look beautiful, Susanna."

The girl smiled and nodded, as if affirming her mother's statement, and then peeled off her sweater and began to get ready.

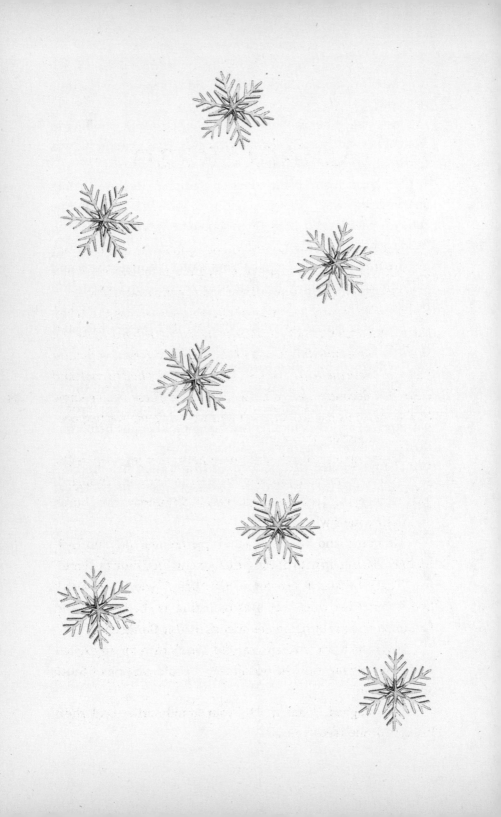

CHAPTER 20

Dinner around the Lunds' kitchen table was cramped but delightful. Josie thought the lasagna was the best she'd had in years, though Arlene swore she hadn't gone to any trouble.

Bless her heart, Josie thought, eyeing her across the table, *she waited until we got here so Susanna could help her make the salad. What wonderful friends we've made lately, even without a house to invite them to ourselves. I used to think I had to cook and clean and decorate, just to have guests over. These people know how to make us feel welcome without worrying and fretting over things that just aren't important.*

"Josie, you and the children have never met Jerry's parents, have you?" Arlene said, interrupting Josie's wandering thoughts. "I'd love it if you all could come over again on Sunday after church and share a meal with us then."

"Grandma and Grandpa Lund are coming on Sunday?" Melody's face lit up with obvious excitement. "You didn't tell me!"

"That's because I just found out today," Arlene answered. She lowered her voice, her eyes twinkling as she spoke. "And Grandma Lund is bringing her famous marble Bundt cake."

This time it was sixteen-year-old Todd's turn for an excited outburst. "My favorite," he exclaimed. "I could eat one of those all by myself!"

Jerry laughed. "Exactly why your grandmother said she'd bring two. She's seen you eat."

Todd's face flushed under his blond hairline, but he laughed good-naturedly at his father's ribbing and shrugged. "I can't help it," he said. "I'm a growing boy."

"Me too," Jacob chimed in.

Josie cut her eyes to her son, who sat next to Todd. The older boy looked down at him. "I've noticed that lately," he said. "You've gotten taller just since I saw you last. I wouldn't be surprised if your muscles have grown too."

Immediately Jacob lifted an arm and flexed his bicep. Todd felt it and nodded. "Yep, I was right. Definitely bigger."

Jacob beamed, and Josie's heart swelled with love for this little gathering of friends and family. It had been so long since she'd felt she belonged somewhere, and now . . .

Now, what? she asked herself, stopping her thoughts before they could run away from her. *Now you think you do? Are you forgetting that you have no husband, no home . . . no sure place for you or your children to lay your heads at night? Don't forget that all this will come to an end very soon, and you'll be right back out on the street, hoping for room in a shelter or enough money for a cheesy motel so you won't have to drag your children back to that alley behind the cleaners at night. Keep it in perspective, Josie girl. These are nice people, but their lives are not the same as yours.*

"So what do you think, Josie?" Arlene asked, pulling the conversation back to her original question. "Can you and the children join us on Sunday? I really would love for all of you to meet Jerry's parents."

"Please, Mommy," Susanna begged, tugging on Josie's sleeve and gazing up at her with wide eyes, misting with tears. "We don't have a grandma anymore. Please?"

Josie felt as if she'd been stabbed through the heart with a jagged bolt of hot lightning. The reminder that her children had never known Josie's father, since he'd died before they were born, nor had they had a relationship with Sam's parents, who lived on the East Coast until they too died a few years earlier, was something she hadn't considered when counting her children's losses. They'd always had her mother, but now the only grandparent they'd ever known was gone, along with their father. There weren't even any aunts or uncles or cousins in the picture. Josie was all her children had. How could she deny them even the smallest of pleasures?

"Sure," she said, moving her gaze from Susanna's pleading face back to Arlene's. "We'll come on Sunday." *But that's it,* she told herself. *On Monday, if the weather's back to normal, we're packing up and leaving Karen's before we get any more entrenched in these people's lives than we already are.*

Susanna was clapping and cheering in her ear, as Jacob asked Todd what a Bundt cake was and the rest of the normal mealtime chatter resumed. Josie entered in just enough to be polite, but already she was planning for their move the following week.

* * *

Rick shook uncontrollably as he huddled against the wall behind the cleaners. Once again he'd given up an available bed to someone he felt was more needy than he. Gratefully he had accepted an extra blanket from the elderly man named Mr. Foley, who sat in a wheelchair and had the unenviable job of telling the last-minute stragglers that there was no room left for them. Rick knew if it were up to Mr. Foley, he'd let people in if they ended up with standing-room only, but there was an ordinance that had to be obeyed if the shelter was to maintain the right to operate.

The extra blanket helped only slightly, but at least the wind had died down some and the snow wasn't falling. Still, the temperatures were expected to dip down into the low twenties, possibly even the teens, before the night was over. It was one of the worst cold spells Rick could remember in a very long time.

"Maybe that's because you weren't as old and feeble then," he told himself, trying to smile. But his beard felt nearly as frozen as his fingers and toes. How much longer before the good Lord called him home? So far as Rick was concerned, it couldn't be soon enough.

Mr. Foley didn't look good, he thought, trying to turn his mind from his own plight. *He might have been bundled up real warm, and I know he'll sleep inside tonight, but . . .*

He shook his head. The old man usually had a good color to him. Tonight he'd just looked gray. Rick was glad he'd had a chance to pray with him before he left. He'd have to be sure to stop by and check on him more often during the next week.

He closed his eyes, pulling the blanket over his head, praying sleep would come. Was that a good idea? After all, a man could freeze to death out here—just go to sleep and never wake up. Then again, God was the one who numbered his days, and Rick knew there couldn't be too many left, regardless of where he slept. He also knew he could trust the One who held him in His nail-scarred hands to take care of him, and so he relaxed and drifted off to sleep.

＊ ＊ ＊

By first light Rick had awakened half a dozen times, getting up to move around at each interval. So far he could still feel his fingers and toes, so he took that to be a good sign.

Squinting up into the sky, he thought, *Another hour at least before they start serving coffee or breakfast anywhere. Maybe I'll just walk around awhile and get the old blood moving.*

Within moments he was overcome with the worst coughing fit he'd had all night, forcing him to his knees on the sidewalk.

This time there was more blood than usual, but he spit it into his handkerchief and waited until he felt strong enough to pull himself back to his feet and set out once again for the nearest shelter where he knew he'd be able to get some hot java soon.

"Oh, Lord," he said aloud, not worrying that anyone might hear him, even if there had been another soul on the empty street, "it has to be soon, right? Soon, Lord."

His walk more of a shuffle now, he forced himself to place one foot in front of the other as he made his way around the corner and toward the spot where he knew the breakfast line would soon be forming. Those who had been fortunate enough to sleep inside were assured of breakfast, but the rest of them just had to hope they got there before the food ran out. Though he hadn't had much of an appetite lately, he imagined it was a good idea to keep his strength up as best he could. He'd really like to make it until Christmas Eve if possible, as there was nothing he liked better than attending a candlelight service.

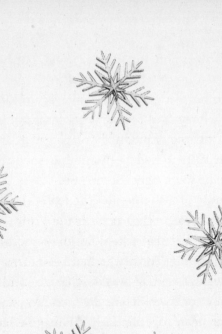

CHAPTER 21

Karen was concerned. Dinner with the Lunds had been a lovely event, but despite the children's obvious enjoyment and enthusiasm, she couldn't help but notice that Josie hung back a bit. It wasn't anything specific that she said or did, but Karen sensed she was troubled by the jovial get-together; she could only hope it didn't preclude a foolish choice on Josie's part.

Today she was working at the food bank at her church, but she planned to stop by a couple of shelters first, hoping to connect with Rick. She knew his health was deteriorating, but when she'd tried calling his cell phone to check on him, her call had gone directly to voice mail. That didn't really surprise her, since he'd told her he'd probably leave it off except for emergencies. He didn't want to use up the prepaid minutes, and he seldom had somewhere to plug it in for a recharge.

She turned the corner and sighed. Even providing a cell phone for homeless people didn't always guarantee communication access.

Karen spotted the first shelter, just a block away. The line was already down the street and around the block, snaking its way forward as cold, hungry people hoped for a warm cup of coffee and something to fill their grumbling stomachs. Was Rick among them?

She didn't see him, but she pulled into a nearby parking space and made her way along the row, smiling and saying good morning as she went. Most ignored her. A few smiled back, and a handful responded with a greeting. One middle-aged man even told her to get in the back of the line like everyone else, but she assured him she wasn't there to eat. His scowl told her he didn't believe her.

At last she arrived at the front of the line, with still no sign of Rick, nor did she see him anywhere in the crowded courtyard. He must be at the shelter a few blocks away.

Resolved to locate him, she hurried back to her car and made the short drive to the alternate shelter. Sure enough, there he was, about midway through the line. She parked and exited her car, keeping her eyes on him as she approached. When he spotted her, he waved.

Was it her imagination, or did he look thinner than when she'd seen him earlier in the week? Something told her the kind old Vietnam vet wouldn't be homeless much longer. She smiled at the thought, knowing there was nothing Rick wanted more than to finally go home.

"Hey there," she called as she neared his spot in line. "I thought I might find you here. How are you doing?"

His face was pale, but so were most faces in this hungry line of people. She noticed he had a couple of blankets wrapped around his shoulders, topping his old green jacket that was his trademark. He hadn't done that until lately, and it confirmed her suspicions that he was failing fast.

"I'm doing OK," he said, his smile taking years off his lined face. "Blessed, actually. How about you, my friend? And Josie and the kids?"

"Fine, too," she said. "All of us are doing well. Little Susanna is feeling much better."

Rick nodded. "Good. I've been praying for them."

"Me too," she said. "So . . . waiting for breakfast, eh?"

He nodded again. "Yep. I came over here instead of the

other shelter because I wanted to check on a friend of mine who volunteers here, and see how he's doing."

Karen raised her eyebrows. "Oh? Who is that? I know a lot of the people here."

"Mr. Foley," Rick answered. "An elderly gentleman in a wheelchair."

Karen smiled. "Yes, absolutely, I do know Mr. Foley. A very nice man."

Rick tugged at his outer blanket and pulled it more tightly around him as the line inched forward. "The last time I saw him he didn't look too good, so I thought I'd come by and see if he's any better today. Maybe pray with him again."

Wasn't that just like Rick, Karen marveled. To be in such poor health himself and yet to be concerned with someone else. Something told her God had a very special place waiting for this goodhearted man when he finally made it home.

"Well, I just wanted to touch base with you," she said. "I'm on my way to the church to do some work over there today. You know you can call me if you need me, right?"

Rick smiled. "I do, thanks. And I will . . . if I need you."

Karen paused and then nodded. "Good. All right, if I don't hear from you before, then I'll plan on seeing you on Sunday for church. Then we're all invited to the Lunds' for Sunday dinner after that—you're included."

"I'll try to make it for church," he said. "Not sure about dinner, though."

The line moved again, and Karen nodded before turning back toward her car, her eyes stinging with unexpected tears.

❄ ❄ ❄

Josie steeled herself as she and the children piled into Karen's car on Sunday morning, along with Rick who jumped at the chance to sit in the back seat with Jacob and Susanna. Though it seemed he did his best to joke and laugh with the kids, she was certain he was pushing himself to do it. He looked thinner and weaker than she remembered, and it seemed to have happened so quickly. Just how sick was he, anyway? She made a mental note to ask Karen that question later that day, after they returned from the Lunds'.

But it wasn't so much Rick's situation that forced her to guard her emotions; it was what she planned to do the next day. She no longer had the excuse of Susanna's health to keep them at Karen's, and the extreme cold snap had finally broken. If they were going to leave — and she was determined they would — Monday was as good a day as any. She'd hold off until then because she'd promised the Lunds they'd come for dinner today and meet Jerry's parents. But that was it. Putting off their leaving wasn't going to make it any easier. Sooner or later they had to go out on their own. Karen had gone far beyond the call of duty to help them. She was the perfect example of the Good Samaritan, but Josie wasn't about to take advantage of her any longer. After all, there were so many others who were homeless and just as needy as she and her family. It wasn't fair for them to take up so much of Karen's time and resources. Besides, the longer they stayed, the more difficult it would be to finally tear her children away.

I've got enough money to get us through the rest of the month now, Josie thought, as Karen steered the car into the church parking lot. *If we're careful and just go to motels when the shelters are full, we shouldn't have to resort to the alley behind the cleaners at all. Maybe by the time January rolls around, we'll be at the top of the list for housing. Oh, please, God, let that happen!*

There she was, praying again. But lately that didn't seem to surprise her as much. And since they were about to go into the church for the morning worship service, it actually felt quite appropriate.

It doesn't have to be anything fancy, God, she prayed as they all climbed out of the car and slammed the doors behind them. *Just somewhere safe, somewhere we can call home, a permanent address . . . Oh, Lord, please!*

"We're here, Mommy," Susanna chirped, slipping her mittened hand into Josie's.

Josie smiled down at her excited daughter. "We sure are, aren't we?"

Susanna nodded, her face aglow, the picture of health.

And Josie prayed again. *Thank You, Lord . . . for healing Susanna. Thank You so very much.*

❄ ❄ ❄

Karen awoke earlier than usual on Monday morning, feeling as if someone had tapped her on the shoulder. She opened her eyes to her still darkened room and blinked. No one was there, of course, but she'd walked with God long enough to recognize that still small voice calling her to communion with Him.

"I'm awake, Lord," she whispered, pulling herself from her warm bed and slipping into her robe and slippers. She stepped to the rocking chair near the foot of her bed and sank down onto the cushioned seat. It was a spot she'd spent many hours talking to her Lord, and she knew she'd be adding to that time this day.

"It's Josie and her children, isn't it, Father?"

Wordlessly, she sensed His affirmation. She closed her eyes and listened, responding at intervals and offering prayers and petitions when they took shape in her heart. By the time she opened her eyes once again, the room was light. Morning had broken, and so had her call to prayer. For now, her business with the Father was finished.

With a brief stop in the bathroom, she headed for the kitchen. Before she could get the coffee brewing, she heard a footfall behind her. She knew it was Josie before she turned around to look.

"Good morning," Josie said, standing in the kitchen doorway, fully dressed.

Karen smiled. "Good morning to you, my friend," she said. "Coffee will be ready soon."

Josie nodded and stepped into the room. "I . . . have something to tell you."

Karen held up her hand. "I already know," she said, holding her smile. "The Father told me you'd be leaving today."

Josie's eyebrows rose. "He . . . told you?"

Karen nodded. "We've had a long talk about you and the kids this morning. I really wish you wouldn't leave, but I understand that you feel you must. So I want you to know I'll be praying for you, and my offer is still open. If you need to come back here for a while, you're always welcome. Just call me. My number is programmed in, remember?"

"I remember." Josie dropped her head. "It's not that we don't like it here," she said, lifting her eyes at last. "You've been wonderful to us. I know the children want to stay. So do I, really, but . . . but that's why we can't. It just . . . hurts too much to get attached."

Karen swallowed. "I imagine it does." She sighed. "Still, I wish you—" She stopped herself. "No, I'm sorry. I promised myself—and the Father—that I wouldn't try to talk you out of this. You've made up your mind, and I will respect your decision. But please, please don't hesitate to call me or come back anytime."

Josie nodded again and then sat down at the table. "I haven't told the kids yet."

"Do you want me to help you?"

She shook her head. "No. I have to do it myself."

Karen paused. "You'll stay long enough for breakfast, won't you?"

Josie looked up. Her smile was thin. "Sure," she said. "I'd like that. Then I'll tell Jacob and Susanna. We'll pack our things and be on our way before lunch."

"Not without a sack full of sandwiches and fruit you won't," Karen said, forcing a chuckle. "And what's left of those Christmas cookies too. The good Lord knows I don't need them."

Josie didn't join in her laughter. "Thank you," she said. "You're so good to us."

Karen turned back to the counter and finished making the coffee. It seemed she just couldn't say anymore at that moment, though the memories of the joyous afternoon they'd all spent together at the Lunds' the previous day danced in her head and tugged at her heart.

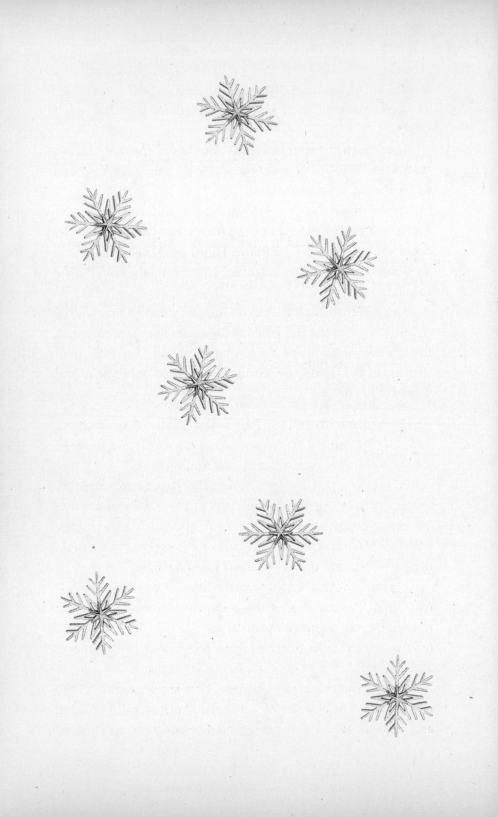

CHAPTER 22

I don't see why we had to leave Miss Karen's house to come to the library," Susanna groused as they trudged up the steps just before noon. "I liked it over there."

Wordlessly, Jacob opened the door and held it as his mother and sister stepped inside. "I've already explained it all to you," Josie whispered, leaning down so her lips would be near Susanna's ear. "We can talk more about it later. For now we're going to get some studying done."

She allowed her eyes to scan the room and was pleased to find it was relatively empty. Their favorite table toward the back and near the computers seemed to beckon them, and Josie led the way, confident that her brood followed.

As she set up the children's books and papers and waited for them to get settled, she glanced toward the front of the room. Louise wasn't there, but then she often wasn't on Mondays. Josie was slightly familiar with the woman who stood behind the desk, talking with a patron, but she didn't know her name.

That's all right, she told herself. *We won't stay too long. Just have lunch, do some studies, and then head on over to the shelter to see if we can get in. If not we'll go to a motel. Either way, we'll have a roof over our heads tonight, and food in our stomach. That's better than a lot of people have, that's for sure.*

Once the children were busy reading, she logged on at the nearest computer and checked her email. Nothing worth reading and certainly nothing that required a response. She'd checked her email a couple of times while they were at Karen's, so she wasn't surprised, though she always hoped to open her account and find something from the county, saying they had housing for her. Apparently not yet.

She sighed and logged out, returning to the table to sit between her children. She would so much prefer for the three of them to be sitting in the warmth and comfort of Karen's home or the Lunds'—or better yet, their own—but she was thankful to have enough to assure food and shelter for the time being.

"I have a question," Susanna said, snagging Josie's attention.

She turned toward her daughter, who stared up at her, eyes squinted and mouth in a determined line. "What is it, honey?" she asked, holding her voice at a whisper so Susanna would do the same.

168   "What about Christmas caroling on Sunday night? The Lunds invited us, and so did Miss Karen. All the kids in our class at church are going."

Josie swallowed, but the lump that had just popped into her throat refused to be dislodged. She knew how much both of the kids had been looking forward to the event.

Before she could answer, Jacob put his hand on her arm. She turned in his direction to find his dark eyes as focused on her as Susanna's blue ones had been. "I want to go, too, Mom."

She nodded, tears pricking her eyes. "And you shall," she said. "I promise. I'll call Miss Karen before then and work things out so you can go."

Jacob held her gaze before nodding his ascent. "Good," he said, turning back to his book. "It wouldn't be fair for us not to go."

It wouldn't be fair indeed. She knew that then, and determined to keep her promise to her children. All three of them would be on that special ride, singing carols this coming

Sunday night as if they had as normal a life as anyone else. And then they'd go to a motel for the night because by that time, all the shelters would be full.

*   *   *

Josie and the kids arrived at the shelter in plenty of time to get in the front part of the line, so she was confident they'd get in for the night. When the doors opened and Mr. Foley rolled out in his wheelchair, Jacob darted to his side, throwing his arms around the man who looked equally pleased to see his little friend.

"Well, well," he said, as they completed their hug and Jacob pulled back, "I sure am glad to see you again. Where have you been?"

"Staying with a friend," he said. "My sister and I really liked it there, but Mom thought we were taking advantage so we had to leave."

Mr. Foley glanced at Josie and smiled before returning his attention to Jacob. "Well, you need to trust your mom's judgment, now, don't you, Jacob? I'm sure she has her reasons."

Jacob shrugged. "I guess."

The old man smiled "Whatever the reason, I'm glad you're here. If it's all right with your mother, why don't you stand here and keep me company while we check people in? What do you think?"

Jacob turned a questioning glance toward Josie, and she nodded. She knew her son had been worried about Mr. Foley, and it would do him good to spend time with him. On the other hand, the old man appeared weaker than the last time she'd seen him. She sure hoped everything was OK.

For now she would just concentrate on getting herself and Susanna inside and finding three cots together for the night. They had eaten some of the food Karen gave them for lunch, and she planned to save the rest for the next day since the shelter would feed them this evening and in the morning.

Another day and night covered, she thought. *Thank You, Lord.*

And she smiled. This praying thing was starting to become a habit again.

❄ ❄ ❄

It had taken every ounce of Rick's strength to drag himself to Karen's on Wednesday evening, but he'd made it in time for a ride to church. He'd been saddened to learn that Josie and the kids had left two days earlier, but he'd climbed into the passenger seat of Karen's car, determined to continue in prayer for the family he had come to care about so very much.

"So they aren't coming to church tonight either then," Rick commented, his statement more of a question.

"I'm afraid not," Karen said, peering over her shoulder as she backed out of the driveway, the windshield wipers already clicking back and forth in the heavy mist. "But she did call and say they'd be here Sunday evening, even if they miss the morning service. The kids aren't about to let Josie back out of that Christmas caroling adventure after church Sunday night."

Rick smiled. "I'm glad," he said, swallowing a cough "I know they're really looking forward to it."

Karen nodded and turned the car in the direction of the church. "How are you feeling these days?"

He glanced at her and saw that her eyes were straight ahead, but her jaw twitched as she awaited his answer. No sense trying any false bravado with her. Karen was too sharp for that.

"Not so good," he admitted. "I think my days on earth are just about over."

She paused before answering, still not turning to look at him. "Have you . . . seen a doctor? Maybe there's something they can do. There are free clinics, you know . . . and emergency rooms."

"That's not the issue," he said. "I have VA benefits, and I could go into a veterans' home somewhere for my last days . . . if I wanted to. But I don't. I'm where I want to be . . . for now. I'll be home soon, and that's all that really matters. To be honest, the sooner God calls me home, the better."

"Somehow that doesn't sound like a death wish."

Rick shook his head. "No, ma'am. It's a longing to go home, to be with the Father, to see Jesus face to face, not to mention my parents and a lot of others who have gone on before me."

He saw her nod once, and he knew she understood.

"Still," she said, "the streets are a tough place to spend your last days. Are you sure you wouldn't rather be somewhere warm and dry? I've heard some of those veterans' home are pretty nice."

Rick used a coughing fit as an excuse to delay his answer. Finally he said, "Not for me. I don't do well in cramped-up spaces, with people hovering over me and medicating me and telling me what to eat and when. Nope, I'm just fine where I am for now."

"All right," Karen said, and he heard the resignation in her voice. "But remember you have that phone. All you have to do is punch the number like I showed you, and it will call me."

Rick grinned and scratched his beard. "I'd have to turn it on first."

Karen slid him a glance and shook her head. "Yes, you would. And you do remember how to do that, right?"

"I do," he said, "and I promise that if I need you, I'll turn on the phone and call you."

She held his gaze for a few more seconds, and then nodded and turned her eyes back to the road in front of them. "Good," she said. "See that you do."

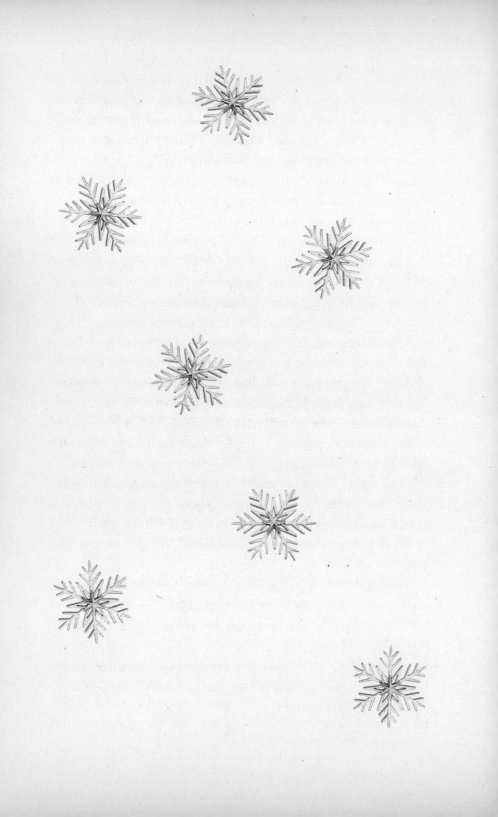

CHAPTER 23

By Sunday Josie and the kids had managed to get into shelters every night except one, which they'd spent in a halfway decent motel. Though they hadn't tried to get to Karen's in time to go to the morning service that day, Josie knew she had no choice but to get them there that evening. Jacob and Susanna had talked about little else all week except going caroling, and she knew they expected her to take them to Karen's house to catch a ride. Meanwhile they'd spent most of the day at the mall since the library was closed.

Around four, as the three of them rested on a bench, Josie turned on her phone and called Karen. "I just wanted to make sure it was OK to come over and catch a ride to church with you," she said. "And, of course, the kids are bursting with excitement about caroling tonight."

Karen laughed, and Josie's heart warmed at the familiar sound. She was surprised at how very special the woman had become to her in such a short time.

"I'm sure they are," Karen said. "And to be honest, so am I! This is one of my favorite events every year. Thankfully it's not supposed to rain, but we'll bring extra blankets to bundle up. Meanwhile, why don't you all head on over here now? I have a roast in the oven, so we can grab something to eat before we go. I'm hoping Rick will join us too."

Rick. The Vietnam vet. Josie's heart tugged at the thought. He had been so good to them, and she knew her children would love seeing him again. "Sure," she said, "if you're sure you don't mind. I mean, we can get something to eat first if—"

"Don't be silly," Karen interrupted. "I didn't fix an entire roast for myself, you know. Do you need me to pick you up?"

Josie shook her head, despite the fact that she knew Karen couldn't see her. "Oh no," she answered. "We're at the mall, right on the bus line, and we can catch one in a few minutes. We'll see you within the hour."

"Perfect. See you then," she said, and clicked off.

Josie returned the phone to her backpack and smiled at the two faces fixed anxiously on hers. "We're going to head on over there now," she explained. "Miss Karen has dinner ready for us, and Rick might even come too. Then we'll all go over to the church after that."

"Yay!" Susanna popped up from her seat and threw her arms in the air. "We're going to Miss Karen's and then Christmas caroling. I can't wait!"

Jacob too stood to his feet, a smile spreading across his face. "And Rick's coming too. Cool!"

"I didn't say that for sure," Josie corrected him. "Karen said she's hoping he'll come."

Jacob's enthusiasm dampened only slightly. "He'll come," he said, picking up his backpack and slinging it over his shoulder. "Let's go. I'm starved!"

"Me too," Susanna added, grabbing her things as well.

Josie laughed. "All right. Two starved children need to eat, and a roast sounds like the perfect solution. Let's go catch that bus."

Weaving their way through the crowded mall, they veered straight toward the nearest exit. Josie almost dared to believe they were going to have a wonderful time, but she had to shove aside her concerns about where they would sleep when the caroling was over. All the shelters would long since be filled, and she wasn't even sure about catching a bus to find a cheap motel at that hour. But they'd just have to deal with that problem when it got there. For now, they were headed to a friend's home for a delicious meal and a fun evening. It was the least she could provide for her children who asked so little of her.

❄ ❄ ❄

As much as they'd enjoyed their dinner and pleasant visiting around Karen's kitchen table, they'd nearly given up on Rick until they heard the faint knock at the front door.

"He's here," Jacob exclaimed, jumping up from his chair and racing to the front room before Josie could say anything about not running in the house. Susanna scurried after him, leaving the two women to smile at each other across the table.

"They love Rick, don't they?" Karen observed.

Josie nodded. "He's been so kind to all of us."

"I'm not surprised."

Marveling, as she had done several times lately, that one who had so little could yet offer so much, Josie smiled as she heard her children's excited voices returning to the kitchen. She didn't doubt that Rick would be in tow.

"Look who's here," Jacob announced as the three of them squeezed through the doorway into the kitchen.

"It's Rick," Susanna said, beaming as if she'd just discovered something wonderful that no one else knew.

Josie smiled up at the bearded man, but her heart constricted at the weariness of his face. Lately it seemed he aged each time she saw him.

"Welcome," Karen said, rising from her seat and grabbing a plate from the cupboard. "Will you join us for some roast? We still have time before we leave."

Rick smiled. "Well, maybe just a little," he said. "Don't seem to have much of an appetite lately, but who can turn down your cooking?"

"It's delicious," Susanna assured him, still clinging to his hand.

He grinned down at her. "I don't doubt that. Come to think of it, I've never had anything to eat here that wasn't."

In moments they were all seated around the table once again, as Rick managed to eat a few small bites of meat, occasionally smiling and nodding at the chatter that flowed among them. But Josie couldn't help but notice that despite his valiant effort, Rick barely made a dent in his meal, not to mention that he had to stop several times to cough into his handkerchief. Did her children realize the extent of Rick's illness? She doubted it, and she worried about how they'd react if he continued to deteriorate.

At last it was time to leave for church, and they all piled into Karen's car, with Rick once again taking the back seat with Susanna and Jacob. Though the children urged him to join them on the caroling trip after the service, Rick declined, saying it would end too late for him to get a bed for the night. That comment brought an immediate offer from Karen for Josie and the children to stay at her place after their outing. Josie initially refused, but Karen wouldn't take no for an answer. It seemed their sleeping situation was resolved for the night, though Josie couldn't help but wonder where Rick would end up.

❄ ❄ ❄

The worship service had touched Rick's heart even more than usual, and he'd found himself completely caught up in the sermon, even as his eyes occasionally drifted to the Advent candles on the altar. There was only one candle remaining to be lit, as well as the main one in the middle, the one signifying the birth of the Christ Child, the entrance of the Light of the world into the godless darkness.

Rick closed his eyes at the thought. *Christmas. You've watched over me for more than sixty of them, Lord, even before I acknowledged or thanked You for it. Well, I'm thanking you for it now. You know there were times when I wondered why You ever created me, but I know I have no right to even think such things. I'm just so grateful You've shown me one last way I can bless others before I come home to You.*

Home. He smiled. *Will I be there in time for Christmas, Father?*

His only answer was the little girl named Susanna, silently slipping her warm hand into his. The feeling of belonging and acceptance transferred the warmth of her tiny hand straight to his heart.

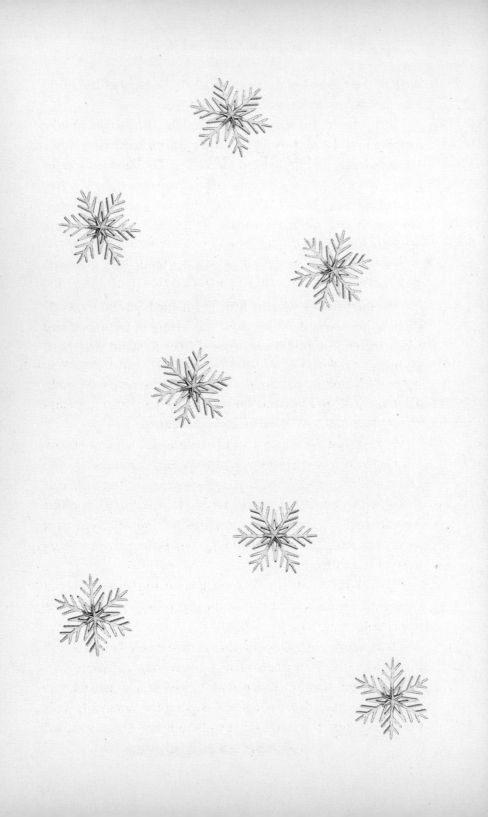

CHAPTER 24

Frigid air nipped at Josie's nose, but she felt more snug and secure than she had in at least a year. Bundled under jackets and quilts, she was pressed against one side of the huge old truck bed, with Susanna on one side and Jacob on the other. Nearly thirty adults and children had piled into the back of the truck, scrunching up as close as possible before the engine cranked to a start and pulled slowly out of the parking lot to begin their preplanned route through nearby neighborhoods. Though Jacob and Susanna had made one last valiant attempt to convince Rick to join them, he had declined.

They'd scarcely gone a block before the singing began. Joining in with gusto, Josie fought tears as she glanced at each of her children. Their cheeks and noses were red, but their eyes shone with excitement. Josie imagined their thoughts didn't contain even a hint of their homeless condition. For tonight, at least, they felt a part of something; they belonged, and Josie's heart ached with gratitude.

"Thank You, God," she whispered, not in the least concerned that anyone would hear her over the joyful singing that poured from the happy group.

They drove slowly enough that people inside houses heard them and came to stand in open doors, waving and some even joining in the singing. When they arrived at a nursing home along the route and stopped in the parking lot, she nearly wept when residents were wheeled outside to listen. Some watched from windows, and Josie recognized the surprised but welcome look that flooded their faces. It so closely mirrored what she felt in her own heart at that moment.

These people from the church, they really do care, she thought. *About God, about one another, about these lonely, elderly people . . . about us — my children and me. Why couldn't I see that before?*

Sam's face floated into view then, and her sense of joy evaporated. In that moment she realized that, deep down, she'd blamed Sam for the fact that she'd walked away from her faith. But was it really his fault? Hadn't she already turned her back on God before she made the decision to marry an unbeliever? She'd been raised in church; she knew better. And yet she'd chosen to follow her feelings, rather than God's Word. Her mother had warned her, but she hadn't listened. She'd been so sure it would all work out. And it had seemed to . . . at least until Sam got sick. Then everything had changed.

The usual angry question that followed that thought, accusing Sam and asking why he hadn't prepared them for what lay ahead, didn't take shape in her mind this time. Instead the vague, guilt-laden heartache that she'd shoved away for months once again began to niggle at her heart. Did she dare allow it entrance into her consciousness at last?

Sam! Oh Sam, where are you now? What happened to your soul after you breathed your last? If you really didn't know Jesus —

"Mommy, your favorite song."

Susanna's voice and tug on her mother's sleeve saved Josie from her silent agony. Gratefully she pulled herself back to the present. She was here now, with her children and with people who cared about them, singing Christmas carols and then going to Karen's to sleep in warm beds afterward. She would revisit the rest tomorrow . . . maybe.

"Silent night," the group sang. "Holy night. All is calm . . . "

Josie swallowed the lump that threatened her and joined in. "All is bright." Oh, if only she could believe the words she sang! She knew she was nearly at the place where she just might at last be able to forgive Sam—and even God. The question now was, could He ever forgive her?

* * *

Karen knew something was up. She'd observed Josie all evening—at church, while they were caroling, and afterward when they came home and sat around the tree before tucking the children in for the night. God was doing something in Josie's heart, and Karen was determined to partner with Him in the process.

The lights were out now, even the colored ones on the tree. Josie and Susanna were in the spare room, and Jacob was sound asleep on the couch. The scene warmed Karen's heart. She loved having the Meyers family here in her home; she just wished she could convince Josie to stay for a while, but the woman had made it quite clear that they were only here for the night. So be it. There was work to do, and Karen was not one to shirk her duties.

Settling down in the comfortable old rocker in her room, she sat in the dark with her favorite quilt wrapped around her. "I'm here, Father," she whispered. "I'm ready to pray, for as long as You want me to, and about anything You wish. I'm sure it has something to do with Josie and her children, so for now I'll just sit with You and listen."

She sighed, a smile touching her lips. Spending time alone with her Father, who was also her Husband, was the best part of Karen's day. Before John died, she'd thought life couldn't get any better than when he came home from work and they shared their evenings together. Now, as wonderful as those times were, she knew they couldn't begin to compare to the time she spent with her Lord. Whether He kept her in prayer for a matter of moments or throughout the night, she anticipated their time of communion with great joy.

Josie, she thought. *How I pray you will one day know the depth of love that can only be shared with God Himself!*

As she meditated on her silent words, she realized that was the perfect place to begin her conversation with God. And so she did.

* * *

Arlene Lund couldn't sleep. She'd been thrilled to realize that Josie and the children were joining the group to go caroling, even though she and Jerry had opted not to go along. Now she lay beside her husband in their queen-sized bed, listening to him snore and thanking God that Josie's family was sleeping at Karen's this night.

You always provide, don't you, Lord? she prayed silently. *You know I was heartbroken when we had to ask that sweet little family to leave, but You already had a plan in place — as You always do. I don't know where You're taking them, Father, or what will happen to them along the way. But I know You're faithful and You love them so much more than I do, so I know Your plan for them is a good one. Thank You for allowing me and my family to be a small part of that.*

She smiled into the darkness, remembering Jacob and Susanna's excitement as they said goodnight in the church parking lot and then scrambled into the back of the truck for their caroling excursion. Watching their energy and enthusiasm just reminded Arlene of how recently her own two had been that age.

I can't even imagine how difficult it would be to raise children without their father, not to mention without a home, she thought. *It's tough enough under the best of circumstances, and Josie certainly hasn't been experiencing many of those lately.*

She closed her eyes, ignoring the teardrops that squeezed outward onto her cheeks. *Please continue to cover and protect and guide them, Lord,* she prayed. *And please, use us—or anyone else who crosses their path—to accomplish Your purposes in their lives.*

❄ ❄ ❄

Rick had been right: all the shelters were long since full by the time he got out of church and made his way back downtown. He hadn't even been able to catch a ride with Karen since she had joined the others on the back of the truck.

Hunkered down against the wall in the alley behind the cleaners, he clutched his blanket and smiled at the memory of Jacob and Susanna, clambering onboard and squishing down with their mom to lean against the side of the truck as they bundled up and headed out onto the street. He'd waved to them one last time as they drove by, but they'd been so busy tuning up their voices and getting ready to launch into their first song that they hadn't even noticed him.

"They're a beautiful family, Lord," he said aloud, glad he had the place to himself. In the dim glow of the pole light from the edge of building, he could just barely see his breath in front of his face. It would be another cold night, but at least not as bad as it had been a week or so earlier. And besides, before long he'd be basking in the warm presence of His Savior, so what was a little temporal discomfort?

"Please take care of them, Father," he said. "Please make sure that everything works out for them once I'm gone."

He nearly laughed at the realization of what he had just said. Did he really think God needed Rick's help to provide for the Meyers family? Of course, that wasn't true, but Rick was pleased that his Lord would allow him to be part of the very special Christmas gift that he knew the family would receive this year.

"Thank You, Lord," he whispered, breaking into a cough. When it subsided at last, he prayed softly, "Hold me, Father, will You? I need You more than ever right now."

The warmth that flowed down from the top of his head to his feet assured him that God had indeed heard and answered his prayers, and with that he drifted off to sleep.

Chapter 25

By the time Josie awoke on Monday morning, the sun was already peeking through the window, and it took her only a moment to remember where they were.

She turned her head and assured herself that Susanna still slept, then raised herself from bed and headed for the bathroom in the hallway. Peeking into the front room on the way, she saw that Jacob too still slept.

Not surprisingly, she thought as she closed the bathroom door behind her. *They had quite a day yesterday!*

She smiled at the memory of sharing a meal around Karen's table, including when Rick arrived to join them, and then heading over to the church. The children had been so excited they'd scarcely been able to sit still through the service. By the time they finally got back to Karen's at the end of the evening, Susanna had declared it "the very best day ever." Though Josie had wrestled momentarily with the ever-present reminder that her children's joy was only temporary and reality would set in quickly the next day, she had still dropped off to sleep nearly as quickly as Susanna and Jacob.

God gives His beloved sleep.

The vague Bible verse, which she imagined she wasn't even remembering correctly, floated through her mind. Her mother had spoken it to her many times when she was little and having trouble sleeping. Funny that she would think of it now . . . or was it?

She glanced into the mirror. Her blonde hair was slightly duller than it had once been, but her eyes were still clear and blue. Sam used to call her his "beauty." Would he still do so if he could see her now?

The pain of the question that had pierced her heart the night before now stabbed her with fresh vigor. Could he see her? Wherever he was, was he aware of his own presence, let alone anyone else's? The thought that he might have died without ever truly receiving Christ was something she had pushed away since it had first occurred to her, but for some reason it now seemed determined to worm its way in, whether she wanted to deal with it or not.

And just how do I deal with such a possibility? she asked herself. The image that stared back at her seemed to offer no answer. Her heart grew heavier as the question hovered over her, accusing and condemning her as she stood, defenseless.

I should have prayed more, she thought. *Should have talked to Sam more about Jesus and told him all the things I learned when I was little. I should have tried to bring him to the truth before it was too late. Oh, Lord, I'm so sorry! Can You ever forgive me?*

Though a quiet assurance in her heart told her that God had indeed forgiven her—for so many things—she doubted she'd ever be able to forgive herself. Tears trickled down her cheeks now, as she stood in front of the mirror, facing for the first time what she had tried to avoid since her husband's death. Was Sam in hell today, this very moment . . . because of her?

She shook her head as if to loose the stronghold of the thought. *Leave me alone,* she wanted to cry aloud. But she didn't because she knew there was no use. The thought had succeeded in invading her consciousness at last, and now there was no getting rid of it. All this time she'd blamed Sam for leaving her, God for allowing him to do so, and the church for not helping her and her children the way she thought they should. But the ugly truth was that it was she who was to blame—she who had denied her faith and failed her husband. The pain was too much to bear. How would she carry it and still care for her children?

I will carry it for you, came the whispered answer. *Just give it to me.*

Josie watched her eyes widen in the mirror. Had God spoken those words to her, or was she just imagining it, clinging to false hope in a desperate attempt to survive?

Swiping at the tears that still dripped from her eyes, she turned on the faucet and leaned down to splash water on her face. She had to get a grip; her children needed her. This was no time to lose control. Maybe God was speaking to her; maybe He wasn't. Either way, she had to do whatever was necessary to care for Jacob and Susanna this day and get them to shelter tonight. Focusing on that immediate need, one day at a time, would get her through and help her forget the tortuous thoughts of what had happened to Sam when he died—as well as her part in his fate. She knew the questions would return, but for now she must ignore them. And that was exactly what she planned to do.

❄ ❄ ❄

Josie couldn't shake the feeling that she was being stalked. She told herself it was ridiculous, but an invisible presence seemed to haunt her every step. Even now, as she and the children rode the bus from Karen's place to the library, she sensed it. The strangest part of it all was that she didn't feel threatened by it.

She shook her head as they arrived at their stop. Helping Susanna and Jacob gather their things as they exited the bus into the cool noonday sun, she told herself she was imagining things.

You're letting your imagination run away with you, Josie Meyers, she scolded silently. *Just way too much emotion getting in the way of sound reasoning. Get a grip, OK? All you have to do is get the kids through the afternoon and then head over to the shelter in time to get in for the night. How hard can that be? You should have it down to a science by now.*

But despite the firm words, she was certain she was being followed—pursued, actually—and she knew it was God Himself who was after her. And that, of course, was the problem. How did one outrun God?

As they approached the familiar steps that led to the library's front doors, she dismissed her thoughts and focused instead on the scenery around her, noticing as if for the first time the bare cherry trees that lined the walkway. Had they always been there? Obviously they had, and in a few more weeks their outstretched branches would be sporting new buds. But for now they looked nearly as forlorn as she felt when she let her mind head in the forbidden direction of Sam's eternal fate.

All the more reason not to go there, she reminded herself. *There's nothing I can do about it now. Sam is dead. He left us destitute, and I have no way of knowing where he's spending eternity. I know he never consciously told me he had accepted Jesus as his Savior, but then again, he never really denied him either.*

Tears bit her eyes, and she shut down the thought before it could take over. *I need to get the kids settled in reading and then sign on to a computer and get my mind on something else. Who knows? Maybe I'll have an email with some good news about our housing.*

But even as she dared to hope that might be the case, she knew better. No way was she going to get housing any time soon. The last time she'd checked there were still more names ahead of hers than she could count. She'd just have to keep taking Susanna and Jacob to shelters and cheap motels and pray the money didn't run out and force them back to sleeping in alleys. If she could do that and keep some sort of food in her children's stomachs, they just might make it after all.

❄ ❄ ❄

The hours at the library had passed uneventfully, though Josie hadn't been very successful at blocking out the thoughts she'd been wrestling with since the previous day. Finally she'd loaded the children back onto the bus and they'd headed for the shelter. She knew the doors wouldn't open for an hour or so, but she wanted to be sure to get in line with time to spare.

"It's cold out here, Mommy," Susanna complained. "Why couldn't we stay at the library a little longer?" Before Josie could answer, her daughter added, "Or at Miss Karen's? She always says we can stay. Why don't we, Mommy? I like it there. I'm tired of being cold and sleeping at shelters."

Josie's heart felt like a block of ice as she squatted down to face her child. As badly as she wanted to dismiss Susanna's questions, she had to admit they were legitimate and deserved an answer.

"I'm sorry, honey," she said, holding the girl's blue-eyed gaze with her own. "I know you like it at Miss Karen's, and so do I. And maybe we'll stay there once in awhile. But like I told you when we stayed with the Lunds, that's not our home. We can't live there, as much as we might want to."

Tears pooled in Susanna's eyes, and her chin quivered. "Why not?" she whined. "It's not fair. Other people have homes. Why can't we?" She stomped her foot, and her voice raised a notch. "I hate being homeless. I hate it!"

Josie felt her cheeks flame, not so much because of what others around her might think, since most probably shared Susanna's feelings, but more because the girl was asking questions Josie couldn't answer and making demands she couldn't meet.

She wiped a tear from Susanna's cheek. "I know, baby. I know you hate it. We all do. But we can't help it right now. We just have to be thankful for shelters and food and friends who take us caroling and help when they can."

Josie watched the war of emotions on the child's face until, at last, her shoulders slumped and she nodded, her chin dipped in resignation. "I know, Mommy," she whispered. "I'm sorry. I just . . . I just wanted to sleep at Miss Karen's tonight instead of standing here in the cold."

Her own eyes stinging with tears, Josie pulled her daughter close, stroking her hair and wishing she could say or do something to change their situation. Obviously that wasn't an option unless she gave into the pressure to stay at Karen's for a while. Was she just being stubborn in refusing to do so? She'd been so sure before, but lately she didn't seem to be sure of anything. The only thing she knew for certain was that she had to outrun the thoughts of Sam and where he had ended up . . . and how she had so completely failed him.

CHAPTER 26

It seemed Josie no sooner got Susanna settled down than Jacob became agitated.

"Look, Mom," he said, pointing toward the front door of the shelter, which had opened just minutes earlier. "Mr. Foley isn't there."

A heavy feeling of dread pressed down on Josie's heart at the implications. Surely nothing had happened to the elderly man since they saw him last! Then again, she'd thought he hadn't looked too well at the time.

Oh, please, God, she prayed silently, even as she forced a weak smile and turned from comforting Susanna to deal with Jacob.

"I'm sure he's just inside somewhere," she said. "Maybe he didn't want to come out in the cold tonight. After all, other people can serve at the front door too. They may have put Mr. Foley to work somewhere else."

Jacob's nod was slow and unsure, and Josie knew he was anything but convinced. But he waited patiently until they stood in front of the gray-haired woman who took names and admitted people to the shelter.

"Where's Mr. Foley?" Jacob blurted the moment the woman looked up at them. "How come he's not here like he usually is?"

The woman's smile faded, and a troubled look clouded her eyes, as she lifted her gaze toward Josie. In that moment Josie knew, and her knees nearly buckled beneath her. She laid a hand on Jacob's shoulder, feeling him tremble beneath her touch.

"Are you . . . friends of Mr. Foley?" she asked.

"Yes," Jacob answered, stiffening under Josie's touch. "We're good friends. Why isn't he here, waiting for us?"

The woman's lip quivered as she answered. "I'm afraid . . . I'm afraid Mr. Foley has passed," she said. "He hasn't been well, you know, and . . . well, just yesterday, his heart gave out. He—"

Jacob dropped to the ground with a wail, and Josie gasped at the suddenness of his reaction. His grief over his father had come more slowly, and certainly less dramatically than this.

As she knelt beside him and tried to pull him into her arms, his wails continued, and she wondered if she was going to be able to calm him enough to get him inside. "Come on, sweetheart," she crooned. "Let's go find a cot, and we can sit down and talk about this, all right?"

Jacob jerked his head up, his dark eyes wild with grief as tears streamed down his red cheeks. "He was my friend," he sobbed. "Mr. Foley was my friend!"

Vice grips seemed to squeeze the blood from Josie's heart as she realized the depth of her son's pain. In addition, Susanna was now whimpering as well.

"Help me, Lord," she whispered, standing to her feet and lifting her son to his. "Take it easy, honey," she said. "We all need to get inside now, all right?"

The lady at the door smiled understandingly, though her forehead was still creased with obvious concern. Josie knew she needed to get her children inside so others could get checked in, and with determined steps through the doorway and a hand on each child, she managed to do so. Once inside, she aimed them straight for three empty cots toward the back of the room. She prayed her son's grieving could be contained enough that he wouldn't keep others awake, but she was at a loss to deal with him at this point since she'd never seen him so emotionally distraught.

Not even when Sam died, she thought. *Dear Lord, what has happened to him . . . and what do I do to help him?*

*　❋　❋　❋*

Josie had finally managed to calm Jacob, though he refused a sandwich when they were handed out.

"You need to eat," Josie had urged him. "You'll be starved before morning if you don't."

"No, I won't," Jacob insisted. "I'm not hungry now and I won't be later either." Tears popped back into his eyes then. "I just want to see Mr. Foley again! Why did he have to die?"

Josie gathered him into her arms once again, rocking him as she did her best to console him. Quite obviously this emotional meltdown was about more than Mr. Foley, though Jacob had certainly taken to the elderly man. But right now he was grieving as he never did when his father died. Perhaps it had all just caught up with him, Josie reasoned. Still, she felt helpless to comfort him, though she prayed silently as she rubbed his back.

At last he fell asleep, sniffling into his jacket, which he had rolled up to use as a pillow. When he quieted and his breathing became deep and regular, Josie too relaxed. Maybe he would be calmer in the morning.

"Mommy?"

Josie had been so busy tending to Jacob that she hadn't realized Susanna was still awake. Moving the few inches between her own cot and her daughter's, she knelt beside Susanna and stroked her hair back from her forehead. "What is it, sweetheart?" she whispered, careful not to disturb the others around them.

"Jacob's sad, isn't he?"

193

Josie sighed. It was an understatement, but a true one nonetheless. "Yes, honey, he is. He liked Mr. Foley a lot."

"So did I."

Josie leaned down and planted a kiss on her daughter's forehead before whispering her answer. "I know you did, baby. I did too. He was a very nice man."

"Is he in heaven now?"

Josie's heart raced. Was Mr. Foley in heaven? She hadn't known him well, but well enough to believe he probably was a Christian. "Yes, honey, I'm sure he is. I believe Mr. Foley loved Jesus, and he's with him now."

"Like Grandma?"

Josie swallowed. "Yes, like Grandma."

Susanna paused before asking the question that Josie was dreading before the words were spoken. "What about Daddy? Is he in heaven with Jesus and Mr. Foley and Grandma?"

A rushing sound whooshed through Josie's ears, and she was certain the room tilted around her. *Slow, deep breaths,* she told herself. *Hold it together for Susanna's sake. She needs the right answer. Don't punish her for your failures.*

"I . . . " She took another deep breath and tried again. "I know you've heard about Jesus and heaven at church, haven't you?"

In the dim light she saw her child nod.

"Good. Then you know that everyone who loves Jesus and accepts him as their Savior goes to heaven when they die, right?"

Susanna nodded again. "But . . . did Daddy love Jesus?"

Josie thought her heart would stop. She fought for air before she was able to take a breath and formulate an answer. But what answer could she give? *Oh Lord, help me!*

"Ask Jesus that question," Josie whispered, wondering where the words had come from. "He'll tell you what you need to know."

"I already did," she said. "A long time ago."

Josie raised her eyebrows. "You did? And what did Jesus tell you?"

"He said to trust Him and that He loves Daddy even more than I do."

Josie felt her shoulders relax, and she smiled. "That's the perfect answer, isn't it?"

Susanna nodded and smiled. "Yep. Jesus is taking care of Daddy now, just like He's taking care of us."

Tears burned in her eyes as Josie pulled her daughter close. "You are so right, Susanna. He surely is."

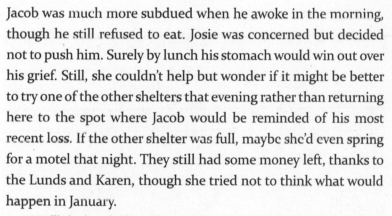

Jacob was much more subdued when he awoke in the morning, though he still refused to eat. Josie was concerned but decided not to push him. Surely by lunch his stomach would win out over his grief. Still, she couldn't help but wonder if it might be better to try one of the other shelters that evening rather than returning here to the spot where Jacob would be reminded of his most recent loss. If the other shelter was full, maybe she'd even spring for a motel that night. They still had some money left, thanks to the Lunds and Karen, though she tried not to think what would happen in January.

We'll deal with that when we get to it, she told herself for the umpteenth time, settling into the middle of a bus seat with a child on each side. The three of them rode quietly as they headed to the library. She'd been relieved to learn Louise would be working all week, so that meant they shouldn't have to worry about being hassled or run off if they spent too much time there. It was the perfect place to spend a quiet day, where the children could read, she could check her emails, they could have their lunch—and above all, they could stay warm, safe, and dry.

And try not to think too much about Mr. Foley . . . or the question Susanna asked me last night. She squeezed her eyes shut. *Oh Lord, if only I knew for sure about Sam! He went to church occasionally, and even prayed once in a while. But . . . did he know You? Did he love You? If he did, he never really showed it. Oh Father, if only I'd been more faithful! Could I have made a difference? Could I have led him to You?*

The only sound she heard in response was the hiss of the airbrakes as the bus pulled to a stop in front of the library. She opened her eyes, took her children by the hand, and led them out the door into the cold, gray morning.

CHAPTER 27

The clouds were back on Tuesday, but thankfully it wasn't raining yet. Rick hadn't slept well and didn't feel hungry at all that morning. As lunch time rolled around, however, he thought maybe he should wander over to the spot at the park where some of the churches occasionally came to distribute sandwiches and blankets and words of encouragement . . . along with prayers and free New Testaments to anyone who wanted them. Rick had once again given away his Bible to someone who seemed to need it more than he, so he hoped to get another one, along with a bologna or peanut butter sandwich.

The six-block trek in the damp weather took him longer than it had just a couple of weeks earlier, but he arrived in time to get in on the lunch and Bible distribution. Tucking his New Testament into his jacket pocket, he patted it and smiled. He appreciated the sandwich, but God's Word was the food he really needed. He planned to spend the rest of the day hunkered down somewhere, reading and praying.

It occurred to him that he could probably go to the library and maybe even run into the Meyers family, since he imagined they'd left Karen's by now. Then again, he wondered if it was good for Jacob and Susanna to see him in his worsening condition.

Will it be any better if they suddenly learn you're gone?

The question zinged him like an arrow to the heart, and he grinned. "You sure have a way of getting my attention, Father," he whispered. "OK, the library it is. Besides, I can't deny that I'd enjoy thawing out for a little while. And I always like seeing those kids. Thanks, Lord."

With that he set out for yet another long, chilly walk, hoping the rain would hold off at least until he got there.

❅ ❅ ❅

Once again Josie felt she had logged into her email account for nothing. Sometimes she wondered why she bothered. She halfheartedly scanned a few job sites, but knew there was no way she was going to find anything that way. Even if by some miracle she did, what would she do with her children while she worked? What would she give as a home address? She did at least have an email address and a cell phone now, but . . .

The cell phone. She hadn't even turned it on since they left Karen's. What if she had a message? She really needed to be more conscientious about checking it a couple of times each day. At least she could recharge it here at the library.

She fumbled in her backpack and retrieved the phone, turned it on, and waited for it to spring to life. But like the emails, there was nothing.

Josie sighed. Sometimes she felt like a non-person. She knew she shouldn't, and times like Sunday night, when she and the children were so welcomed and included in the caroling activities, she truly felt as if they belonged. But today, camped out at the library while she waited for yet another day to pass before returning to the shelter in hopes of getting in for the night, her identity felt shaky at best.

"Mommy!"

The loud whisper snagged her attention, and she turned to the nearby table where her children sat. Jacob was smiling, his gaze aimed at the entrance, while Susanna's eyes were fixed on her mother. Grinning, she said, "Rick's here. Look!"

Josie turned toward the front, and sure enough, there was the familiar Vietnam vet with the gray beard and lined face, smiling at her children as he shuffled toward them. Was it just her imagination, or was his gait much slower and less steady even than it had been on Sunday evening when they last saw him? No, she was sure of it. And he was still losing weight.

She rose from her seat and stepped to the table where Jacob and Susanna waited, arriving at the same time as Rick. As they exchanged greetings, she couldn't help but notice his face was nearly as gray as his hair and beard. His brown eyes had lost their sparkle and seemed sunken, but his smile was as warm as ever.

Oh, Lord, he doesn't look good, she thought, even as they invited him to join them at their table. She thought of the meager lunch she'd picked up at a convenience store on the way over—a pre-packaged sandwich for each of them and three bananas. It was scarcely enough for her and the children, but she imagined she could get by without eating until they returned to the shelter that night.

"I'm so glad you got here when you did," she said, keeping her voice down but making sure to inject a note of enthusiasm into it. "We were about to eat lunch." She dug into her backpack and pulled out the food, handing a sandwich and piece of fruit to Rick. "You can join us."

Rick held up his hands and shook his head. "Oh, no," he said. "I already ate. I just came from the park where they were handing out sandwiches. But thanks anyway. You all go ahead and eat, though." He dug in his pocket then and pulled out a small black book. "I also got this with my sandwich. Isn't that great?"

Once again the old vet's eyes were sparkling, and Josie's heart warmed. This man's faith was no collection of empty words or sayings; he believed it, and he lived it. Despite his homeless

199

condition, Josie realized at that moment that Rick was richer than most people she had known in her lifetime.

With the children happily chewing on their sandwiches, Rick opened his new treasure and, in a hushed but reverent voice, began reading the Christmas story from the Gospel of Luke. Within a few heartbeats Josie realized she no longer felt like a non-person. By this simple act, Rick had reminded her of her identity as a child of God, and at that moment, nothing else mattered.

❄ ❄ ❄

By late afternoon Josie knew they needed to board the bus and head back to the shelter if they were going to be assured of a place to stay for the night. She was determined to hold off on spending money on motels unless she had no choice. At least that way she'd be assured of having enough on Christmas Eve if the shelters filled up that night, which she'd heard often happened. There was no way she was going to allow her children to sleep on the street on Christmas.

As they packed up their things and headed for the library exit, Josie caught Louise's eye and offered a quick wave and a smile. No doubt her friend knew they'd be back tomorrow.

Rick accompanied them as far as the bus stop and bid them farewell and turned to leave.

"Aren't you coming with us?" Susanna asked, frowning.

The man whose shoulders appeared much more hunched than Josie remembered paused, turning back slowly and smiling as he gazed down at the child's upturned face. "I might see you over there," he said, and then shrugged. "I'm not much for busses. I'd rather walk."

"But . . . " Susanna paused before continuing. "But it's starting to rain. And it's cold. Why don't you ride with us?"

Josie realized then that Rick either didn't have bus fare or was reticent to spend whatever money he might have. She spoke up quickly before he could respond to Susanna.

"She's right," Josie said. "Why not ride with us? We have extra bus tokens—just got them this morning, as a matter of fact. It would mean a lot to us if you would."

Her eyes held his, and though she knew he was aware of what she was doing, she also knew he would agree for the children's sake.

At last he nodded. "Sure," he said. "Why not? I guess it won't kill me to ride the bus just this once."

Susanna clapped her hands in delight and then threw her arms around the startled man's legs. Josie imagined he wasn't used to such displays of affection, but she was certain he enjoyed it. Jacob too was beaming as they huddled together, waiting for their transportation, which was scheduled to arrive momentarily.

"Thanks," Josie said, leaning toward Rick and keeping her voice low.

Rick smiled but kept his eyes fixed on the bus that had just lumbered into sight.

By the time they were aboard and settled into the very back row of seats where they could all sit together, Josie found herself wondering again about Rick's health. It was obviously deteriorating. Surely as a veteran he could get some medical help somewhere . . . couldn't he?

"Do you know that Mr. Foley died?"

Jacob's question cut through Josie's thoughts, startling her back to the present. A quick glance at her son told her he had posed his question directly to Rick, who now gazed down at him, all vestiges of a smile having melted away.

"I did," he said. "I heard about it at the park earlier today, when the churches were distributing lunch. A lot of people knew and loved him. He'll be missed."

Jacob's dark eyes brimmed with tears, and he nodded. "He was my friend," he said, his soft voice cracking with emotion.

Rick reached out his hand to cover Jacob's. "He was my friend too," he said. "And I'm glad he knew Jesus. That means we'll see him again, you know."

The air crackled between them as Josie waited for her son's response. At last he nodded again. "Yeah. I know that," he said. "And my grandma too."

The words that should have comforted Josie's heart instead pierced her soul with renewed guilt. Though Jacob was comforted knowing he would see his grandmother and Mr. Foley again, he hadn't mentioned his father. And once again, Josie was brought full circle to the questions that haunted her.

Yes, she'd had a conversation with Susanna that seemed, at least for the time, to have answered the question of Sam Meyers' eternal destiny. But now her doubts had returned. Would she ever find forgiveness and peace with this issue, or would she live in torment for the rest of her life?

Turning to look out the window in an effort to hide her tears, Josie scolded herself for her emotional weakness and instability. How could she swing between such extremes? Just a short time ago she'd listened to Rick reading from the Scriptures and had felt such peace. Now that peace was gone, replaced by a sense of hopelessness and self-loathing. How could she ever raise her children to have a healthy outlook on life when her own was so very skewed?

CHAPTER 28

The line leading to the entrance to the shelter was already halfway down the block when they arrived. Josie's stomach clenched. Had they waited too long? Would they end up going to a motel after all?

Rick stood with them as they waited for the doors to open and the check-in process to begin, battling two coughing bouts in the process. She couldn't help but notice the concern on her children's faces as the man turned away from them to cough into his handkerchief. As hard as Jacob had taken Mr. Foley's death, how would he or Susanna cope with the loss of this man named Rick who had become so dear to them in such a short time? For there was little doubt in her mind that the weary Vietnam vet would not survive the winter—and the thought sent her to shivering as she tugged her jacket tighter against the cold mist that fell from the gray sky.

At last the doors opened and the line began to inch its way forward. The same gray-haired woman who had been there the night before now manned the entrance, taking names and admitting people into the warmth of the shelter. Already Josie's stomach was growling in anticipation of the nightly sandwich that went with the cot, and she prayed they would indeed make it inside before the doors were closed for the night.

The winter darkness that enveloped the Pacific Northwest by late afternoon was nearly complete by the time Josie, Rick, and the children stepped up to the doorway. The woman smiled in recognition, wrote down their names, and nodded at them to go inside.

Rick hesitated. "Are you nearly full?" he asked. "Because if you are, I can go somewhere else." He glanced behind him at the many people still waiting in line. "There are a lot of women and children back there who need a bed more than I do."

The woman smiled. "We have plenty of room left," she said. "I don't foresee turning any of these folks away tonight, so go on in and get warm. Sandwiches are on the way."

Josie saw a flicker of relief pass over Rick's face before he nodded and turned to follow them inside. She breathed a sigh of relief to know all four of them would sleep in a warm, dry spot this night. If anyone needed or deserved it, surely it was Rick.

❄ ❄ ❄

It was well into the night before the disturbance began. Josie and the children were sleeping soundly, as was most everyone in the shelter, when loud, angry voices jerked her from her slumber.

"You'd better get away from my bed before I call the police!"

The woman's threat reverberated through the room, followed by a screeching retort. "Oh, yeah? How you gonna call them? You got a bullhorn in your pocket, 'cause you sure don't have a phone!"

Josie sat up and zeroed in on the source of the argument. It was coming from just two rows away, where two middle-aged women faced each other down across an empty cot. A wide-eyed audience watched and listened from all corners of the vast room.

The first woman, whose wild red hair seemed to be on fire, appeared momentarily confused at the challenge of how she would summon the police, but it didn't stop her for long. With a howl she lunged across the cot, latching on to the other woman's long dark hair and nearly landing on top of her as they both tumbled to the floor, knocking against several other occupied cots in the process.

Everyone near the two now-wrestling women quickly moved back from the altercation, though their gaze never shifted. Josie too grabbed her children, by then wide awake and clinging to her, and skirted back a few rows to avoid any danger that might come their way.

"What's going on?" she whispered to Rick, who had hurried to their side and stepped between them and the brawling women.

"It's all right," he said, his voice hushed in an obvious attempt to calm Susanna and Jacob. "The redhead is known for making trouble. Sometimes they don't let her into the shelters for just that reason, but other times she's fine—so long as no one provokes her. Apparently the other woman did. Maybe she got too close to her cot or something. She doesn't like anyone invading her space."

Josie's heart hammered against her ribs as she watched a couple of men attempting to break things up, but the women weren't making it easy on them. Two more men had to jump in before the brawlers could be separated, and even then the men came away with a couple of scratches. The women were still hollering and hissing at one another as they were escorted to the door and out into the cold, dark night.

"In all the nights we've spent in shelters, we've never seen anything like that," Josie said, her eyes searching Rick's for an answer. "What in the world was all that about?"

Rick shook his head. "It happens," he said. "The fact you haven't seen it yet is surprising when you consider that quite a few homeless people have mental problems and most are doing without necessary medications." He sighed, scratching his beard as he spoke. "I'm just glad no one was hurt."

"But . . . what will happen to those women now?"

He paused, a look of sadness washing over his face. "Best-case scenario? They'll find somewhere to bed down outside.

Then again, they may start fighting all over again. But one of the volunteers here will have already alerted the police, so they'll no doubt cruise by and check it out. Who knows? Maybe they'll arrest them and they'll find themselves sleeping in a nice warm jail cell tonight. Might be the best thing for both of them."

Jail . . . the best thing? As bad as things had been over the past year, Josie couldn't imagine being so desperate that being arrested could be viewed as a good thing.

Thanking Rick for his help, she and the children said goodnight as he returned to his cot on the other side of the room and Josie got her children settled into theirs. She just hoped they could get back to sleep before morning . . . and avoid any nightmares in the process.

Rick watched as Josie and her children prepared for the day. He hoped they'd been able to get back to sleep after the night's drama, and that they hadn't been too traumatized by it. Though his own mental problems paled in the light of what some endured, his heart ached for anyone who had to deal with such issues, particularly without shelter or protection or medication. It was a horror few could understand.

But today was a new day—no doubt another cold and drizzly one, but at least no snow and ice as they'd had the previous week. As much as he'd enjoyed hanging out with the Meyers family at the library the previous day, he sensed it would be better to part ways with them today. He didn't want the children becoming too attached or dependent on him, knowing how short his time was. Besides, they didn't need to waste their bus tokens on him. He could walk wherever he needed to go, even if it did take him a lot longer than it used to.

Ah, but wait a minute. As he headed for the exit and the light breakfast that awaited him there, he remembered it was Wednesday. If he intended to make a point of not seeing Josie and the kids for a while, he'd have to skip church tonight, as there was always the chance they'd show up there. And church was the one thing he looked forward to from one day to the next. Well, he'd just have to pray about it and see what God had in mind. He always knew best, and Rick had long since learned to follow His lead.

With that in mind, he stepped out into the gray day, gratefully received his donut and juice, and slowly began making his way toward the street. He wasn't sure where he would go once he got there, but at least he knew it would be in the opposite direction of the library. A dry spot where he could sit and read his New Testament was really all he needed, and he trusted that God would lead him to one shortly.

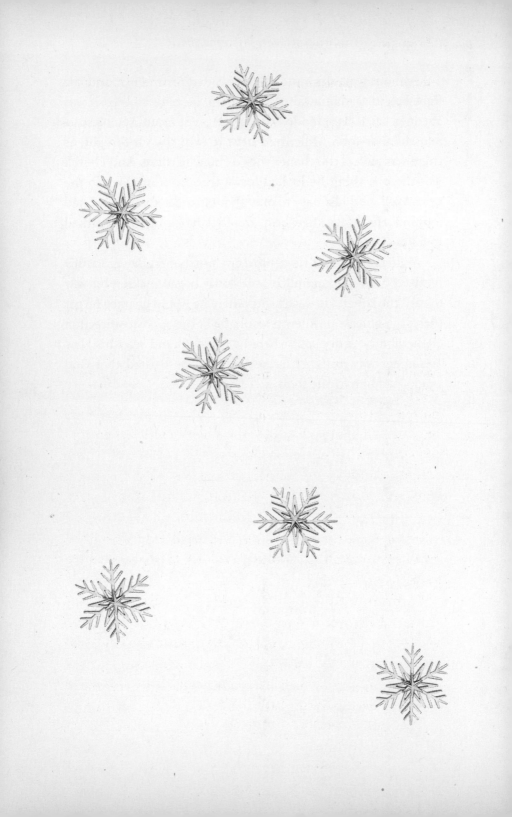

CHAPTER 29

"How come we couldn't go to church tonight?"

It was the second time Susanna had posed the question, and Josie sighed. She knew her children loved being at church, and she had truly wanted to go herself, but she'd been so disturbed over what had happened at the shelter the night before that she'd chosen to splurge on a halfway decent motel for the night. Unfortunately there were none near enough to the church to walk and she didn't want to spend any more money or bus tokens than necessary. And so they'd picked up a small box of pre-nuked chicken from a convenience store and checked into a room before dark. They sat together on the double bed now, munching their dinner and watching cartoons.

"I know you wanted to go to church," Josie said. "And I've already explained to you why we couldn't. We'll go for sure on Sunday morning, all right?"

"But I wanted to see Miss Karen . . . and the Lunds and my friends from my class."

It was obvious Susanna wasn't going to let this go easily.

"Sweetheart," Josie said, "I've tried to explain this the best I can, but sometimes you just have to accept what I tell you, even if you don't like it or understand it."

Susanna's eyes dropped before she looked back up. "Because you're the mommy?"

Josie swallowed a smile. "Yes. Because I'm the mommy."

That seemed to settle the issue, at least for now, and they went back to their dinner. Jacob, however, had his own concerns that apparently he felt needed to be voiced.

"What about Rick? Do you think he went to church? He probably caught a ride with Miss Karen, right? He usually does."

Josie turned her attention to her serious-looking son. His dark eyes were sincere, and she knew he was truly concerned about his friend. "I'm sure he did," she said. "And I'm sure Miss Karen let him know why we weren't there. I called and let her know we weren't coming, remember?"

Jacob nodded. Josie knew he was worried about more than whether or not Rick had been able to ride to church with Karen; he was concerned about Rick's health, as she was. The man was obviously failing, but there was nothing they could do about it.

You could pray.

The words whispered to her from a tiny corner of her heart, surprising her with their intensity. Was that God's way of nudging her? Even as she asked herself the question, she knew the answer.

She smiled at Jacob. "Do you think we should pray for Rick?"

The boy's eyes widened. "Could we?"

"I don't see why not."

"I want to pray too," Susanna chimed in.

Josie smiled. "We'll all pray together," she said, intimidated at the thought but determined to follow through. She gathered up the remains of their dinner and set it on the stand beside the bed, then took her children's hands in her own. "Shall we take turns?" she asked.

When both children agreed, she said, "I'll begin, and then Jacob, you can go next, and then Susanna. All right?"

Once again she received an enthusiastic response, and she closed her eyes. Where and how should she start?

What's in your heart?

The question brought a smile to her lips, and she began. "Dear Lord . . . " And as the words began to flow, she wondered why it had taken her so long to do for her children what her mother had always done for her.

❄ ❄ ❄

Karen was more concerned than ever over Rick's deteriorating health. She knew what a struggle it had been for him to get to her place in order to hitch a ride to church, but he'd been determined, and he'd made it. But it had broken her heart to leave him off downtown afterward.

"Are you sure you won't reconsider?" she'd asked as he opened the door to climb out. "You're welcome to sleep on the back porch or even in the car. Either would be warmer than the street."

Rick had smiled. "Nah. I'm fine. Really. The weather's cold and drippy, but not as icy as it was a few nights ago. And besides, I just ask the Father to wrap me in His arms and keep me warm and safe while I sleep, and He always does."

He paused, and Karen sensed he was fighting his emotions. She waited.

"I'm getting to the point where my times alone with Him are so special that I'm just not willing to give them up—even for shelter. Does that make sense?"

Strangely, it did, and Karen couldn't think of another argument to offer. She smiled. "I'll be praying for you, my friend. And you know I'm just a phone call away if you change your mind."

Rick smiled, nodded, and slammed the door shut behind him. She watched him disappear into the damp night, and her heart ached, but not so much with pity as with admiration for a man who walked so closely to the God he loved.

✳ ✳ ✳

Josie woke early on Thursday morning. The children were still sleeping, so she decided to take a quick shower before rousing Susanna and Jacob. Once they were up, she'd take them for a quick breakfast somewhere and then catch a bus for the library. Tonight they'd be sure to get to the shelter in time to get inside so she wouldn't have to spend anymore money on motels. She knew she couldn't avoid shelters just because of the disturbance she'd witnessed at the last one, but she'd needed a break before returning. When they did, would that same woman be there? Josie hadn't seen her before, so maybe there wouldn't be a repeat performance.

Shame on me for thinking that way, she thought, as she adjusted the shower faucet and got ready to step inside. *The poor woman has it so much harder than I do. To be homeless and unable to think clearly . . . I can't even imagine how hard that must be. Forgive me, Lord, and please help that woman.*

The realization that praying was once again becoming a habit, one she hadn't practiced since she was a child, brought a smile to her lips as she stepped into the small tiled stall. *At least this place has warm water,* she thought, as she stood under the spray. *Funny how much more I appreciate the simpler things in life these days.*

By the time she was out and dressed, the children were stirring.

"I'm hungry," Jacob called.

"I want to watch cartoons," Susanna added.

Josie smiled and shook her head, stepping out of the bathroom to confront her tousle-haired offspring. "You can watch cartoons for thirty minutes," she said to Susanna. "No more, understand?"

Susanna nodded, grinning as she clicked the remote and the TV sprang to life.

Josie turned her attention to Jacob. "I'm hungry too," she said. "Why don't you take your turn in the bathroom before Susanna? When you're both ready we'll head down to the convenience store at the corner and get some breakfast. Sound good?"

Jacob nodded and headed for the bathroom, as Susanna settled down under the covers to enjoy her program. Josie busied herself gathering their things and was feeling good about the day that lay ahead of them until she heard a commercial for yet another Christmas toy.

No wonder I take them to the library every chance I get, instead of the mall. All they see there are the things they'd like to have but can't. Will I ever be able to buy Christmas gifts for my children again? Better yet, will we ever have a tree to put them under or a house of our own to celebrate in?

213

Tears threatened, as did the lump in her throat, but she set her jaw and determined to ignore them. Right now she needed to focus on keeping her little family warm, dry, fed, and safe. So far, though it hadn't been easy, those needs seemed to be met, and she was grateful. The rest really didn't matter that much anyway.

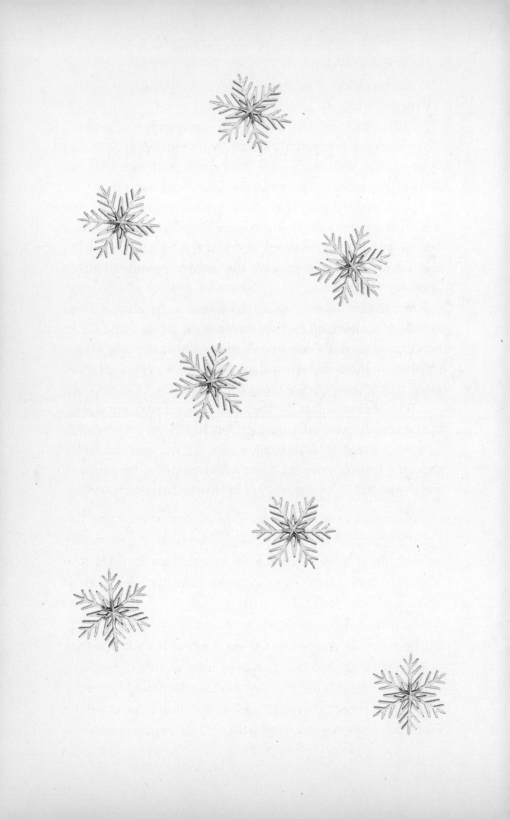

CHAPTER 30

The next few days passed uneventfully, with Josie and her children spending their days at the library and their nights in shelters, but thankfully with no more experiences like the one they'd had with the two women fighting. Still, Josie hadn't been able to shake the memory, and she had come to the conclusion that maybe God let her see it so she'd pray for those involved.

Whoever thought I'd be praying for strangers? She smiled at the thought, as she sat at the familiar table at the library on the day before Christmas Eve, her children on either side of her, engrossed in their books. *For years I didn't even pray for myself or my family unless there seemed to be some sort of emergency. Now You have me praying for people I don't even know. You really are amazing, do You know that, God?*

For an instant she imagined God smiling in response. Yes, He was amazing, and yes, He certainly knew that. It was she who needed the reminder. Who would have thought it would take months of living on the street to get her attention back where it needed to be?

A flash of memory pierced her heart, as she thought of the Christmases she and Sam had spent together in their beautiful home, watching their children grow from infants to toddlers, and beyond. It still hurt terribly to think Sam wouldn't get to see Jacob or Susanna become teenagers or adults, but somehow Josie knew she was going to have to come to the place where she could be grateful for the years they did have together, rather than regretting the ones they wouldn't.

And I need to stop being angry at Sam for leaving us in this situation, don't I, Lord? But I need Your help to do that—and to forgive myself too. Tears bit her eyes then, but she blinked them back. Somehow she knew the forgiving herself part was going to be the hardest. Originally she'd turned most of her anger on God, but she was fairly certain she'd let go of that by now. Could He help her let go of her anger toward Sam and herself? She certainly hoped so, because if He didn't she feared she just might sink down so far into that anger that she'd never find her way out.

All the more reason to make sure I get the children to Christmas Eve service tomorrow evening. I'll rent the motel room first, just to be sure we have somewhere to sleep after church, and then I'll call Karen and let her know we're coming over to go to the service with her. Jacob and Susanna will love that! She frowned, realizing they hadn't seen Rick in several days and hoping he'd show up at Karen's to go the candlelight service with them. *Please, Lord, let him be all right! It sure would be nice to have him join us tomorrow evening.*

❄ ❄ ❄

Rick awoke on Christmas Eve morning, huddled against the wall behind the cleaners, the sweet memory of heavenly choirs echoing in his ears. Had it been only a dream . . . or was God allowing him a little foretaste of what was surely coming soon?

He smiled as he struggled to pull himself to his feet. It was getting harder and harder to force one foot in front of the other, and sometimes he wondered why he bothered. Today was surely one of those days.

As a coughing spasm sliced through his chest, he leaned his back against the wall, balancing as best he could until he regained control. If it weren't that the cleaners would be opening up in a couple of hours, he'd just slide back down the wall and curl up beside it for the remainder of the day. He wasn't hungry at all, so there was no sense forcing himself to walk to the shelter. Then again, where else could he go to spend the day? It wasn't raining at the moment, but the saturated clouds overhead promised a deluge before the day was over.

The temptation to take Karen up on her offer and give her a call was a fleeting one. He dismissed it as quickly as it came. Karen no doubt had lots going on today and sure didn't need him hanging around.

He fumbled in the pocket of his old green jacket and found a few worn dollar bills—enough for a cup of coffee and a donut. Though he doubted he could eat them, he knew a nearby diner where the owner didn't hassle the homeless who came in to kill a few hours, so long as they bought something while they were there. Rick figured he could nurse a cup of coffee and a donut for several hours while he took care of some last-minute business.

Better do it while I still can, he thought to himself, smiling as he realized he now had a reason to force himself to walk a couple of blocks. *Those angel voices are calling me, but I know God has one more thing He wants me to do before I come home, and I sure don't want to show up on His doorstep with unfinished business trailing along behind me.*

❄ ❄ ❄

Christmas Eve. Josie wasn't at all surprised when it was the first thought that filled her children's minds that morning, but it grieved her to think she would have no gifts for them. Still, they had slept in the shelter that night and were now happily munching on a special breakfast of scrambled eggs and sausage, provided by the shelter volunteers. As Josie and her family sat side-by-side with the other shelter residents, around the tables that filled the courtyard, bundled up against the cold and glad the rain seemed to be holding off for a while, she smiled.

It could be a lot worse, she thought, watching Susanna sip her juice and Jacob practically inhale the sausage from his paper plate. *We haven't had to sleep outside since before Thanksgiving—and I know that's thanks to You, Lord. We'll splurge on a motel tonight and then go with Karen to church and then to the Lunds' place to celebrate around their tree. What fun!*

Fun. The very word had become foreign to Josie this past year, but she was thrilled to realize it was back in her vocabulary, even if on a limited basis. Her children needed fun once in awhile, and they needed to experience it in the context of people who cared about them and who honored God in their lives.

That's what keeps the fun in proper perspective, isn't it, Lord? She sipped her black coffee and nodded in agreement with her own thoughts. *How did I ever let myself become so materialistic that I thought life was all about "stuff"—what I bought or used or thought I needed?* She nearly laughed aloud at the realization of how very little she actually needed. Life had indeed changed over the past year—in some ways, for the better.

"Mommy?"

Susanna's voice interrupted Josie's thoughts, and she turned to look at her daughter. "Will we have presents when we go to the Lunds' house after church tonight?"

Josie raised her eyebrows. She'd wondered that herself and imagined they would, but she wasn't going to give her children false hopes. They'd experienced enough disappointments in their short lives.

"I don't know, honey," she said honestly. "We might, but even if we don't, we'll still have a wonderful time there, don't you think."

Susanna nodded. "Yes!" She grinned and scrunched her shoulders up toward her face. "I'm so excited!"

Josie laughed. "I must admit, I am too." She turned toward Jacob, who had stopped shoveling food into his mouth to listen to the conversation. "How about you?" she asked.

His mouth still full, Jacob smiled and swallowed. "Yep," he said, wiping his mouth with his jacket sleeve. "It's going to be great—especially if Rick comes." The shine in his dark eyes dulled only slightly. "Do you think he will?"

The first negative emotion of the day pierced Josie's heart, momentarily deflating her joy. "I don't know," she said. "I asked Karen when I talked to her yesterday, but she wasn't sure either." She laid a hand on Jacob's shoulder. "I'm sure he'll be there if he can."

Jacob nodded and turned his attention back to his breakfast, but Josie noticed he ate with less enthusiasm than before.

What would happen if Rick didn't appear for their Christmas Eve celebration? She knew he seldom missed church, and she couldn't imagine his not coming on Christmas Eve—unless he couldn't help it. She suppressed a shudder at the thought.

Help him, Lord, she prayed silently. *You know where he is. Keep him safe and warm—and if at all possible, please let him join us tonight. It would mean so much to all of us.*

The image of Rick's kind smile filled her mind, even as she heard a whisper in her heart: *Rick is safe in my hands, exactly where he needs to be. Don't worry. Just trust Me.*

Josie smiled. Yes, Rick was fine . . . and they would be too. All she had to do was trust God. Though she'd failed miserably at that for most of her life, she was learning more about it with every passing day.

CHAPTER 31

Josie hadn't realized the library would be closed today, but she chided herself on not considering that possibility. Now they'd wasted bus fare to get there and couldn't get inside. It was far too early to go to Karen's, and far too cold to spend the remainder of the day outside. It looked like the mall was their only option.

It'll be a zoo again, she thought. *All the last-minute shoppers racing around, trying to snatch up a few bargains and cross off the last of the names on their list. Sam was always one of those last-minute guys, looking for great gifts at great prices just hours before Christmas morning.*

The thought squeezed her heart and filled her throat with the lump that never quite went away completely, but she pushed it all back, determined to keep the day upbeat for her children. "Well," she said, "it looks like we won't be spending the day at the library after all. How about if we head over to the mall instead? It's only a few blocks, and it's not raining. We can walk and then hang out there and watch the shopping frenzy. Maybe I'll even treat us all to a hot pretzel or something. What do you say?"

The cheers were immediate, as the children envisioned a real Christmas treat in the warmth of the mall. Despite the change in plans, it looked as if it would be a good day after all.

By the time they arrived, their cheeks and noses were rosy but their spirits high. Josie made a mental note to leave the mall early enough to catch a bus to a decent motel, where she'd rent a room and then, as planned, call Karen to tell them where they were. She'd promised to pick them up as soon as she heard from them and bring them to her place, where they would all have a light supper before heading out to church and then over to the Lunds' house for hot chocolate and cookies. Josie realized she was looking forward to this special Christmas Eve celebration nearly as much as her children.

Once inside, the threesome worked hard at sticking together as they wormed their way through the crowds. As promised, Josie splurged for pretzels and even hot cider for lunch. It took awhile to find a spot where they could sit down to eat, but at last a bench opened up at the far side of the food court, and they all plunked down together. Josie's back was aching a bit, so she slid her backpack off and placed it under the bench, with the kids following her lead.

Within moments they were enjoying one of the tastiest lunches they'd had in awhile. Josie knew pretzels and cider might not be the healthiest food around, but it was delicious. Besides, they needed a special treat occasionally.

People continued to stream in front and behind them, heading in all directions, carrying bags and boxes and chattering excitedly. Josie enjoyed watching them, pondering at times what their personal stories might be. She wondered if anyone glanced at her and her children and guessed at what was going on in their lives.

By mid-afternoon, Susanna was getting sleepy, and Josie decided it was time to get going. Maybe they could check into a motel and catch a short nap before heading for Karen's. It would certainly assure a more pleasant disposition for the children, though she doubted that would be an issue tonight.

As they stood to their feet, they reached under the bench to retrieve their backpacks. Jacob and Susanna snagged theirs immediately, but Josie didn't see hers. As panic rose up in her chest, she dropped to her knees and peered under the bench, as if willing the missing backpack to appear. It didn't, and she realized what had happened. One of the shoppers, passing behind them, had snagged it and walked off with it—along with her cell phone and all the money she had in the world.

Christmas Eve was upon them, and her worst fear was materializing in front of her eyes—no money, no phone, no way to rent a room or even get to a shelter or call Karen. What would they do now?

When the stinging tears bit her eyes, she didn't even try to hold them back. Just when she'd thought things were taking a turn for the better, the world caved in upon her—and God, as usual, had abandoned them.

❄ ❄ ❄

Karen paced between the stove, the table, and the refrigerator. The kitchen was small and didn't offer much room for such activity, but right now she just couldn't possibly sit still. Though she forced herself to continue baking for the night's festivities, her heart and mind were elsewhere. Why hadn't Josie called? She and the children should have been settled in at a motel somewhere by now. Karen had planned her food preparation in a way that would allow her to take an hour away to pick up the Meyers family and bring them back home with her, but she couldn't do that until Josie called and told her where they were. Why hadn't she done that by now?

The knot in her stomach grew as she paced, praying all the while. "Where are they, Father?" she'd ask, time and again, chiding herself for her lack of faith. "I know their whereabouts are no mystery to you, but they are to me, and I surely would appreciate it if you'd share that information with me, Lord." She paused to grab a potholder and cracked the oven door to peek at the cookies. Another couple of minutes and they'd be perfect.

She sighed. Who cared about cookies when a woman and two small children were somewhere outside in the cold? Oh, why hadn't she insisted on picking them up yesterday when she had Josie on the phone? It would have been so much better all the way around.

"Not to mention that I haven't heard from Rick either," she said, returning to her pacing. "Lord, what is with these people? Don't they know how to turn on a phone and punch a pre-programmed number? I made it as easy on them as I could, didn't I?"

She shook her head. "Forgive me, Lord. I'm getting critical now, and I don't mean to be. I'm just worried—and yes, I know, I'm not supposed to worry. I know You're in control, but . . . but a little reassurance would really be nice. Please, Father?"

The strains of "The First Noel," the special ring-tone she'd downloaded just a few days earlier, bounced to life from the cell phone on the table, and Karen nearly jumped in the air as she turned toward the sound and grabbed the device from its spot.

"Hello?" she sputtered. "Josie? Rick? Who is this? Where are you? What happened? Why didn't you call sooner?"

But the voice at the other end wasn't Josie's or Rick's. In fact, it was a voice she only vaguely recognized, and her heart sank as she listened to the news that was the last thing she would have hoped to hear on this eve of the celebration of the Savior's birth.

*   *   *

After the initial shock and devastation of realizing she'd had nearly everything of worth in her stolen backpack—including her cell, money, food vouchers, phone numbers, and identification—Josie had fought the impulse to give up at last, to curl up in a fetal position on the bench at the mall, and just quit. She knew they'd haul her away somewhere and no doubt place her children in foster care, but perhaps that would be best for them after all. Look where staying with her had gotten them—homeless, penniless, hopeless. And on Christmas Eve, of all days.

But even as the shock of what had happened began to sink in and she was able to verbalize their loss to the children, she heard their words of encouragement. Instead of sinking into despair, they begged her to find a way to get hold of Karen or the Lunds.

"They'll help us," Jacob assured her, trying to lift her to her feet. "You know they will."

Josie imagined he was right, but how was she to reach them? She had no phone, no money to use a pay phone or to catch a bus to their home. She hadn't even memorized their numbers! How would she connect with them? Karen was probably waiting for her call right now, wondering what had happened to them. If Karen didn't hear from them soon, she'd probably think Josie had changed her mind and they weren't coming.

"Mommy," Susanna said, kneeling next to Josie and speaking into her ear, "we could pray."

Anger battled with hope as her little girl's innocent suggestion danced through her mind. *We could pray.* True. But hadn't she already tried that? And look where it had gotten them.

Still, what other options did they have? She could ask someone to call the police so she could report the theft, but what good would that do? An officer might come and take the report, but she knew she'd never see that backpack or its contents again. A homeless woman's belongings were hardly a priority for law enforcement. And she just might jeopardize her custody of the children.

Sighing, she pulled herself up and took a deep breath. This was no time for a meltdown. If ever her children needed her, it was right now. And if prayer was their only option, then despite the fact that she was nearly certain it would do no good, they'd give it their best try.

Plunking back down on the bench, she pulled the children down beside her and took their hands. She began with a brief, halting prayer of her own, then waited as each of the children offered one as well.

You probably won't listen to me, she thought, directing her silent accusation at God, *but maybe the children . . . please?*

The answer was clear and immediate, nearly knocking Josie from the bench in its power. *Go to the shelter.*

She frowned. The shelter they went to most often was in the opposite direction of Karen's house. Wouldn't it make more sense to go directly to her friend's place? Then again, what if Karen wasn't home? If she wasn't able to connect with either Karen or the Lunds that night, then the shelter was their only option. And if that's where they were going to go, then they'd better get there soon, before it filled up. The last thing she wanted was for her and the children to end up behind the cleaners on Christmas Eve.

"Let's go," she said, grabbing their hands. "We're going to go to the shelter and make sure we can get in tonight."

"But it's Christmas Eve," Susanna whined. "We're supposed to go to church with Miss Karen and then to the Lunds' house."

Josie peered down at her daughter, summoning her most loving but authoritative expression. "Susanna, this is one of those times that you're just going to have to do what I tell you because . . . "

"Because you're the mommy?"

Josie nodded. "Yes. Because I'm the mommy. And because that's what God told Mommy to do."

Susanna's blue eyes widened. "OK, Mommy."

226

The three of them turned then, hurrying to the mall exit. It would be a long, cold walk to the shelter, but they'd make it before dark if they didn't stop along the way.

She set her pace to enable the children to keep up, but kept them moving in the right direction. As expected, they arrived at dusk, only to find the line stretched around the block. Did this mean they wouldn't get inside after all?

As others continued to arrive and fall into line behind them, Josie did her best to concentrate on getting her children into the shelter, rather than thinking about all she had lost. She glanced down at her left hand and wrist. Maybe it was time to break down and sell her wedding ring and watch after all. But even the pawn shops were closed until the day after Christmas. *Oh, why wasn't I more careful? Why did I take my backpack off and set it where I couldn't see it? I never do that!* But the self-condemnation did nothing but depress her, so she shoved it away. If they could just get through tonight and tomorrow, then they could set about doing whatever needed to be done to get her I.D. replaced and to ensure they would still receive their January check and food vouchers. They'd just have to survive in shelters until then.

Is that why You told me to come here, God?

No answer echoed in her ears, as it had earlier, but a voice behind her nearly jolted her heart from her rib cage.

"Josie! Josie, is that you?"

She and her children spun around at the same time, as squeals of "Miss Karen!" erupted from the children's mouths. Miss Karen indeed! Their beloved friend had found them—and she looked nearly as relieved as Josie felt.

Jacob and Susanna flew into Karen's arms, and in moments the four of them were chattering about what had happened.

"How did you know where to find us?" Josie said at last.

227

Karen shook her head. "I didn't," she admitted, "though each time I prayed I sensed that I should come here first. I'm so glad I did! I just knew something was wrong when you didn't call."

"I should have called sooner—before I lost my phone," Josie said. "I'm usually so careful about my backpack, but . . . "

Karen held up her hand. "No need to explain. These things happen. I'm just glad we found each other."

"God told Mommy to come here," Susanna said, beaming up at Karen. "So here we are!"

Karen's eyes widened, and then she broke into a smile. "Well," she said, "no wonder we connected. I'm sure glad your mommy listened to God."

"Me too," Susanna agreed.

"All right," Karen said, "now that we're all together, let's jump in the car and head over to my house. Supper is waiting, and then there's the church service and our visit with the Lunds. Come on now. We haven't any time to waste."

Josie hesitated. "But . . . you don't understand. If we leave now we won't get a place in the shelter. And . . . and I have no money for a motel."

Karen frowned. "Josie, please, listen to me. I understand your reluctance to let your children get too attached at a place where they can't stay forever, but this is Christmas Eve. There is no way in this world that I'm going to let you all stay in a shelter . . . or even a motel, for that matter. You're coming home with me for the night—and for as long as you need a place to stay—and that's that. Now, no more arguments. Just get in the car."

As Susanna and Jacob squealed and raced toward the vehicle parked at the curb, Karen laid a restraining hand on Josie's arm. "We need to talk," she said. "As soon as we get to my place and get the kids settled down for supper. It's about . . . Rick."

The look in Karen's eyes took Josie's breath away, and she knew what the news would be. How would she ever tell the children? She decided in that moment that she would not tell them until after Christmas, regardless of how many times they asked about their friend or his whereabouts.

* * *

The children were no sooner sitting at Karen's table, eating a light supper of soup and sandwiches, than the two women excused themselves and retreated to Karen's room.

"Rick's gone," Karen said, as they sat together on the edge of her bed. "I got a call from a mutual friend this afternoon, a chaplain who works with the homeless. Rick died in a booth at a little diner where he was sitting, having coffee and a donut earlier today."

Josie felt as if a brick had crashed onto her chest, squeezing the very blood from her heart. Though she'd expected Karen to tell her Rick had died, she'd held out the slimmest of hope that he hadn't. Now he was gone—another loss for her children to absorb. However would she tell them?

"There's more," Karen said. "A few days ago he gave me a large envelope and asked me to keep it for him. He said that when he died, he wanted me to give it to you, that he'd made sure everything was in order—whatever that means." She got up and crossed to her dresser, where she opened the top drawer and pulled out an envelope stuffed with papers. Then she turned and held it out to Josie. "I have no idea what it is. I've never opened it. But it seems appropriate somehow that you would receive it on Christmas Eve."

Trembling, Josie took the envelope from her friend. What could it be? Before she could open it to find out, Karen reached into her pants pocket and pulled out three more pieces of paper, all small and neatly folded. "These were in his possession when he died. Seems he'd just written them this morning, before . . . before he went home to be with Jesus."

The familiar hot tears and lump in her throat were back, and Josie nodded as she took the folded papers. One had her name on it, one had Susanna's, and one Jacob's. The dear man had left them each a note before he died. It was more than Josie could absorb, and she sat there, speechless, as Karen put her arm around her and held her close.

"Will you . . . stay with me while I open the big envelope?" Josie asked.

"Of course."

Still trembling, Josie ripped open the envelope and reached inside, where she found some official looking papers with a small handwritten note attached to the front with a single paperclip.

"Dear Josie Meyers," she read aloud, her voice shaking. "This is my life insurance policy, which I've had since I was in the military. I took out the maximum allowable at the time, even though it cost quite a bit more than the military covered, and somehow I've managed to scrape together the premiums every month. But I wanted to be sure to provide for my family if anything happened to me. As it turned out, I now have no family to leave it to—except you and your children. God showed me that you're the ones He intended this money for, so I gladly sign it over to you and pray God will direct you to the home He has picked out for you. This should be enough to get you a nice little place and have a little left over for emergencies besides. Know that it's a gift from my heart, and I'm honored to be able to leave something behind that will bless someone else. Until I see you all again in heaven, I am your friend and brother in Christ, Rick Johnson."

Josie was weeping by the time she read to the end of the note. "Rick Johnson," she whispered. "Karen, until this moment I never even knew his last name."

Karen patted her shoulder. "It doesn't matter," she said. "God knows. And now Rick knows the Lord as up-close-and-personal as God has known him all these years—the way we'll know Him when it's our turn to go home."

"Home," Josie said, turning to fix her eyes on her friend. "God used Rick to give us a home . . . before he took him home to heaven."

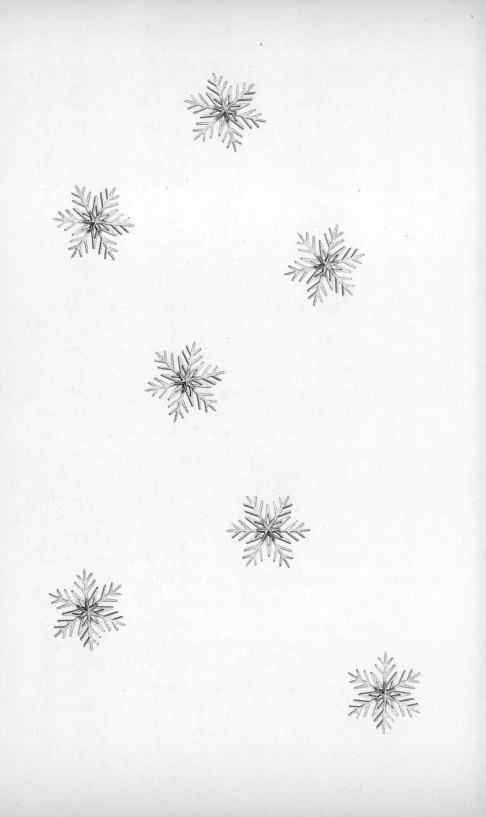

Epilogue

A hesitant knock on the door interrupted their exchange. "Mommy?" Susanna called. "We're done eating. Can we come in?"

Josie took a deep breath, grabbed a tissue from the nearby bed stand, and called out, "Of course, honey. Come on in."

The door opened slowly, and two anxious faces appeared in the doorway. Their expressions turned to concern as their mother's red-rimmed eyes came into focus, but Josie held out her arms and motioned them to come. "I have wonderful news for you," she said. "I can't give you all the details yet, but . . . " She pulled back enough to look them in the eyes as she spoke. "But God has given us an amazing gift this Christmas."

The children's expressions reflected their surprise and excitement as she pressed ahead, determined to share only as much as necessary without telling them about Rick until later. "He's provided us with enough money to get a house—a real house of our very own! What do you think about that?"

Their eruptions of squeals and shouts told her exactly what they thought about it, and she wondered if she'd ever be able to settle them down long enough to give them their notes from Rick. She'd hesitated to do so initially, until she'd realized Rick would not have said anything to them about his impending death. He was just too selfless a man. And so she held out the notes with their names on them.

"These are from Rick," she said. "He . . . couldn't make it tonight, but he wanted to be sure you got these."

Jacob's brief, upward glance told her he suspected something, but he took the paper and unfolded it, reading the brief message aloud. "Dear Jacob, I hope this is the best Christmas ever for you — not because you get lots of presents or candy or anything like that. But because you realize what Christmas really is — God coming to you, shining light in your darkness, pouring love into your heart, and asking you to do the same for others. That's what life is all about, son. Don't ever forget it. Love, Rick."

None of them said a word, as Jacob continued to stare at his note. At last Susanna spoke up. "Read mine, Mommy," she demanded, shoving her note back into Josie's hand. "What does it say? What did Rick write to me?"

Josie looked down at the unfolded paper and cleared her throat. "Dear Susanna, I want you always to remember what a special girl you are. God made you that way, and He has something very special for you to do with your life. Nothing else will make you as happy as doing what He wants you to do. Have a wonderful Christmas — every day of every year! Love, Rick."

Karen and Josie were both sniffling by that time, and even Jacob's chin was trembling. "This is my favorite Christmas present ever," he said, a note of awe in his voice. "I'm going to keep it forever."

"Me, too," Susanna added. "Rick's my Christmas hero!"

As the children turned and rushed from the room, clutching their notes in their hands and chattering excitedly, Josie's eyes fell on the folded paper still sitting in her lap, the one that read "Josie Meyers" on it. Whatever could that dear man say to her that he hadn't already said?

Carefully she unfolded the paper and began to read, stopping several times to clear her throat and swipe at the tears that coursed down her cheeks. "Dear Josie Meyers, always remember that you are a good mother. More than that, I know you were a good wife, too, even though you might think you weren't. I didn't know your husband or anything about him, but I know he must have been a good man to marry you and to have such great kids with you. Most important, I've prayed a lot about him because I know it was hard for you and the kids when he died. God assured me that He loved your husband very much and had the whole situation under control. So if you're carrying any guilt from the past—something you said or didn't say, or should have done and didn't, anything at all—let it go. Your husband's death didn't catch God by surprise, even if it did for you. And now it's time to let it go. Find out what God has for you now, my friend, because as surely as He's forgiven your past, He's also planned your future. And He promises that it's a good one. See you on the other side! Rick."

Karen's arm around her shoulder tightened, as Josie felt the years of pain and guilt wash away with the tears that flowed from her eyes. Thanks to the words of a man who had no home but the one he now enjoyed in heaven, she knew she could finally forgive not only God and her husband . . . but herself.

She lifted her head and smiled up at Karen. "Susanna's not the only one who thinks Rick's a hero," she whispered.

Karen nodded, as Josie's heart swelled with the realization that she and her children were home for Christmas at last—and so was Rick.

THE END

New Hope® Publishers is a division of WMU®, an international organization that challenges Christian believers to understand and be radically involved in God's mission. For more information about WMU, go to wmu.com. More information about New Hope books may be found at NewHopeDigital.com. New Hope books may be purchased at your local bookstore.

Use the QR reader on your
smartphone to visit us online at
NewHopeDigital.com

If you've been blessed by this book, we would like to hear your story.
The publisher and author welcome your comments and
suggestions at: newhopereader@wmu.org.

FREEDOM SERIES BOOK #1

Deliver Me From Evil
ISBN-13: 978-1-59669-306-7
$14.99

Available in bookstores everywhere.

Praise for Deliver Me From Evil...

"Macias tackles one of our world's most perplexing social issues with intense realism and hope. *Deliver Us from Evil* reveals depth, honesty, and grace to guide readers toward a deeper faith and a heart challenged to make a difference in our world."
— **Dillon Burroughs**, activist and coauthor of *Not in My Town*

"*Deliver Me from Evil* will grip your mind and heart from the opening chapter and refuse to let go till you reluctantly close the back cover. Kathi Macias tackles a dark and difficult issue with compelling, complex characters and vivid prose. This novel will change you."
— **James L. Rubart**, best-selling author of *Rooms, Book of Days,* and *The Chair*

For information about these books or any New Hope product, visit NewHopeDigitalcom